Diablo –
Hero of the Night

Gabi Adam

Diablo –
Hero of the Night

ISBN 82-591-1163-2

*For Kim, who brought me home safely
on a foggy night.*

Chapter 1

What a day!

Since early morning, dark storm-driven clouds had been moving across the sky. Rain pelted the fields and meadows, and 13-year-old Ricki Sulai began to wonder if the horses should be let out to the paddock at all in the next few days. As far as she could see from her window, the puddles were already several inches deep out there.

"Darn it," she said aloud to herself, as she watched the large green plastic watering can being blown across the Sulais' yard by the high winds.

The storm howled, seeming to blow through every single crack in the old farmhouse that Ricki's parents had bought not too long ago.

Ricki jumped as a bright flash of lightning lit up the gray sky. A few seconds later, a loud clap of thunder, so near it practically shook the house, sent a cold shiver of fear running down her back.

As a small child she had seen lightning strike a house, and then watched the house burn to the ground. Ever since, she'd had a deep respect for this force of nature.

"It's rare to have rain first and then lightning afterward," commented her boyfriend, Kevin Thomas, who was sitting cozily on Ricki's bed reading the latest issue of *Horse and Rider* magazine.

"Hmm," Ricki murmured, her mind on her horse.

I wonder if Diablo is scared, too, she thought. After all, horses are pretty sensitive to noise, and they usually notice in advance if the weather is about to turn bad.

Ricki kept staring out the window. She would have liked to run over to the stable to see how the horses were doing, but the lightning bolts were coming quickly now, one after the other, so for the moment she decided against it.

Her friends Lillian Bates and Cathy Sutherland lay on their stomachs on the thick white wooly rug that covered the floor between the desk and the closet.

"Racehorse...seven letters...second letter is an R," mumbled Lillian to herself as she stared at a half-finished crossword puzzle.

"Arabian," responded Cathy, who was only half listening. She was concentrating on drawing a portrait of her foster horse, Rashid, from a photo.

Ricki paced nervously from one window to the other. "I don't feel good about this weather," she said, turning to her friends.

"Oh, come on, it's not that bad," said Kevin.

"But the horses..."

"The horses are in a wonderful, dry stable, and they probably have no idea what's going on in the world outside," Lillian completed her friend's sentence. "They're too busy eating."

Ricki kept shifting uneasily from foot to foot. She was so restless she couldn't stand still.

"Today you're like a racehorse at the starting gate, just

waiting for the signal to run," Cathy observed, and threw down her pencil. "Stupid," she said, before she sat up.

"I am not stupid!"

"No, not you! I mean this picture. I just can't get it right! In my drawing Rashid always looks like a cross between a llama and a fox terrier!" she sighed, and then she crumpled up the paper and threw it into the wastepaper basket, which was filling up with Cathy's discarded sketches made during the afternoon.

"Do you guys want to go to the stable with me? I feel as though the ceiling here in my bedroom is about to fall on my head." Ricki looked at each of them in turn.

"I'll go with you. I'm not going to finish anything today anyway," said Cathy spontaneously as she stood up.

"Okay." Lillian got up lazily as well. Kevin was the only one who remained sitting.

"You'll be soaking wet before you get there," he said.

"There are umbrellas!" Ricki replied.

The boy grinned. "Haven't you heard that umbrellas make perfect conductors for lightning?"

"Man, you are a grinch!" Ricki grabbed the closest pillow and threw it at her boyfriend. Immediately, a wild pillow fight broke out.

"What *are* you kids doing in there? Things are shaking so hard the ceiling lamp in the living room is about to fall down!" Ricki's mother, Brigitte, stuck her head in the doorway.

"That's not us, Mom, it's the thunder that makes everything vibrate like that," explained Ricki, out of breath.

"It's going to thunder in your room in a minute if you don't calm down," Brigitte warned with a stern look, and then she turned and left, leaving Ricki and her friends alone.

7

"What's wrong with your mother today?" asked Lillian, surprised. "I've never seen her like this before."

Ricki shrugged her shoulders. "I have no idea," she answered. "But when she makes a face like that, it's not a good sign. Are we going to go to the stable now?" she asked.

"Yeah," three different voices replied in unison.

*

"Yuck, this is horrible." Ricki got to the stable first and hurried to open the door so that she could get inside.

Diablo's head flung upward. He'd been dozing, but when he heard his friend's voice, he was awake in an instant. He whinnied his greeting to her loudly. No matter how often she came into the stable during the day, Diablo's welcome was always so enthusiastic; it was as if he hadn't seen her for months.

"Well, my sweetie, is everything okay?" Ricki walked over to the black horse's stall and pulled his beautiful head down toward her. Gently, she stroked the white star on his forehead that peeked out from underneath the long mane.

Lillian went over to her snow-white Doc Holliday and to Chico, her little donkey, who was standing next to the large Hanoverian, in order to give them both some treats.

"Do you have any extra?" asked Kevin and held out his hand. "Sharazan, that greedy boy, ate all of his two hours ago!"

The long-legged roan sniffed his owner from top to bottom as Kevin opened the stall door, and seemed disappointed that Kevin hadn't brought him anything.

"There are some carrots over here that Carlotta forgot

8

after her last visit," Cathy called from the tack room before she went to her foster horse. "Rashid will be glad to share some of them," she said, ignoring the reproachful look of the tan horse.

I'd have preferred eating them all myself, his look seemed to say. Cathy, however, was already distributing the vitamin-rich treats evenly among the four-legged creatures in the stable.

Rashid, who now belonged to Carlotta Mancini, a former circus equestrienne, used to belong to a small traveling circus and perform with Sharazan. Chico had belonged to the same circus. Lillian's father, Dave Bates, had saved the little donkey from an uncertain future, and Ricki's young brother, Harry, was ecstatic now that Chico resided in his parents' stable.

"What are you all doing here?" asked the dripping wet, black-shrouded elderly man who had suddenly appeared standing in the stable corridor.

"Hi, Jake," grinned Ricki. "We just wanted to check on the horses in this horrible weather. Hey, where in the world did you get that raincoat and hat? You look really spooky."

The old stable master fumbled out of the black slicker and storm hat. He had given Diablo to Ricki months before, after buying for one dollar from an abusive owner the horse he raised from a colt. After this generous gift, Jake Alcott had become an honorary member of Ricki's family. He even lived in a small cottage on the Sulais' property.

"I've had this get-up for at least 40 years," he answered, shaking the rain off his coat and hanging it on a hook outside one of the stalls.

"Well, it looks like it," burst out Kevin.

The old man regarded Kevin, whose clothes were soaking wet, with a disapproving look. Giving him a good once-over, Jake mumbled casually, "I'll bet you would've been glad to have this coat today, wouldn't you?"

Kevin laughed. "You're right, Jake! If Ricki hadn't had the crazy idea of checking on the horses, just because of this storm, I'd have been dry and cozy over there in the house, reading."

"You can't overdo looking after the horses," said Jake, and winked at Ricki. "During a storm like this, horses can often become restless and spooked. I've seen horses break out of their stalls in a panic and create total chaos in the stable."

"Well, our four-legged friends don't seem to mind this storm," answered Kevin. He glanced over at Sharazan, who was calmly munching on a bale of hay.

"Don't kid yourself," warned Jake. "Within a few seconds horses can become wildly dangerous if they panic!"

"Well, you wild thing, you'd better be careful that you don't get a belly-ache from eating all that hay," laughed Kevin as he stroked Sharazan along his neck.

"You should take that seriously, young man! I've spent my whole life with horses, and I know what I'm talking about!" Jake walked slowly into the tack room and opened the food bin.

"Well, as long as you're here, you might as well make yourselves useful," he said. "Come here, Cathy. You can distribute the oats and a little booster feed. Ricki and Lillian…go up to the hayloft and throw down a few bales. And Kevin, you could help me clean out the stalls."

"Aye, aye, Captain!" the kids shouted in chorus and got to work. Jake was glad that he had so much help today. On damp days like this, his old bones always acted up and limited his ability to get around easily.

10

It's terrible to be old, Jake found himself thinking more and more often. But he was determined to do this stable work for as long as he possibly could. After all, he had enjoyed it his entire life.

*

Ricki and Lillian had just climbed the ladder to the hayloft when a tremendous thunderclap was heard and suddenly all the lights in the stable went out.

"Gosh, I can't see anything," said Ricki, crouching down immediately. She wasn't going to budge an inch in this darkness. Once she had stepped into a hole and fallen directly below onto the floor in front of Diablo's stall. Her horse had looked astonished, and even now, whenever she remembered it, every bone in her body began to ache.

Ricki looked around, but she couldn't recognize anything.

"You'd think it was the middle of the night," she said, but Lillian didn't answer.

"Lily?" Ricki listened intently, but…

"Hoo, Hoo!" she heard behind her, and Ricki screamed.

"Man, are you nuts?"

"Scaredy-cat!" Lillian laughed. "If this scares you, how are you going to go on that night ride we signed up for?"

Ricki's heart was still beating wildly.

"Well, first of all, the night ride is planned for a full moon…and I'm not afraid of the dark, I'm just scared of thunderstorms."

"Oh," grinned Lillian. The lights had begun to flicker on again.

Relieved, Ricki took a relaxing breath. Quickly the girls

began to throw down the bales of hay and straw that Jake had asked for. Then they hurried down the ladder before the lights could go out again.

"What was that just now?" asked Ricki. Kevin simply shrugged his shoulders.

"Probably the lightning struck an electric cable somewhere," he replied nonchalantly. Ricki wished Kevin wasn't so laid back about everything all the time.

"Aren't you afraid of anything?" she asked, looking anxiously at him.

"Nope. I've never had any reason to be afraid." He put his arms around his girlfriend to console her and gave her a kiss on the cheek.

"I have a really good guardian angel," he added, and then he got back to work.

"I hope the night ride doesn't get canceled," said Lillian, thinking about her conversation with Ricki in the loft.

"Oh, the weather will be great," commented Cathy optimistically. She cut open the bales of hay that the girls had thrown down from the loft.

"I think it'll be fantastic!" said Kevin. Ricki noticed that his eyes were glowing with excitement just thinking about it.

"I'm glad we could talk your mother into letting you go," said Lillian, glancing at Ricki.

The girl nodded.

"You can't imagine what I have to listen to from her, now that we've settled on a date for the ride: 'Promise me you'll stay with the others the whole time. Don't even think about going off on your own, otherwise you'll get lost. What if Diablo stumbles and you break your neck in the dead of night? Why can't you just ride during the day?

Take a flashlight with you, you never know.'" Ricki imitated her mother's voice and groaned piteously.

"Maybe you should just open a saddle bag and stuff your mother inside," chortled Cathy, and the others joined in her laughter.

Jake was the only one who wasn't amused.

"Well, I think Brigitte's right. Why do you have to ride at night? Night rides are always dangerous…for the horses, because they can't see where they're stepping, and for the riders, too. Sometimes they get lost or even hit by cars because the drivers can't see them in time…or —"

"Aw, Jake, don't be such a spoil sport." Kevin tried to calm the old man down. "You're ruining it for us with all these scary stories. I think Ziggy and Robby from the riding academy took all that into consideration when they were planning the ride. I'm sure they've chosen a completely safe trail, and they'll make certain that we all get home safely."

"You shouldn't be too sure about that," replied Jake solemnly. "They won't be able to catch you if you fall, or prevent the horses from spooking suddenly for some reason and bolting off into the darkness. Even if adults are going with you, you are responsible for yourselves and your horses, and you have to understand that. If I were you, I'd rethink the wisdom of this adventure."

The teenagers looked at each other knowingly.

They should have known that their parents and the old stableman wouldn't be in favor of such activities. Typical.

Ricki was the only one who began to consider what Jake had just said. She knew only too well from experience how quickly an accident could happen.

Earlier in the summer, when Diablo had recovered from

13

an injury to his pastern joint, she and Lillian had taken their horses for a walk. A loud, shrill alarm set off on purpose by a jealous cousin of their friend Josh caused Diablo to panic, lose his footing, and fall. As a result, he got caught in barbed wire and ripped open his flesh in several places. Dr. Hofer had stitched him back together, but Diablo couldn't be ridden for quite a while. But thank goodness the wounds completely healed and Ricki could once again ride through the countryside on her beloved black horse.

Lost in thought, she glanced at her Diablo. She noticed the several rough patches on his coat, especially around his neck. The scars from the stitches that Dr. Hofer had made were still visible.

Thinking about what Jake had said, Ricki began to have second thoughts about whether she should take another risk with her horse. Maybe it would be better not to take part in the night ride. She didn't want anything to happen to her horse ever again.

"Hey, are you dreaming?" Kevin tapped his girlfriend cautiously on the shoulder.

"No," responded Ricki absently, and automatically stepped aside to give him room to push the wheelbarrow past her in the corridor. She kept looking at her horse. She never wanted to experience anything like that again. The memory of Diablo lying on the ground torn and bloody, and her fear that her horse might be dead, still tormented her.

Still deep in thought, she walked over to her horse and observed him, happily eating his hay. He looked up at her with his wonderful shiny eyes.

"Thank God you're completely well again," she whispered to him softly. She decided to reconsider her decision about taking part in the night ride.

*

That night Ricki slept very uneasily. She tossed and turned, her mind racing and her thoughts a jumble.

Sometime during the night she awoke and sat up covered in sweat. Her heart racing wildly, she got out of bed and went to open her bedroom window. She leaned way out and breathed the cool air deeply into her lungs.

For a long moment she closed her eyes and let the coolness of the night calm and refresh her. She tried to imagine what it would be like riding through the countryside on a night like this. Would the experience be a happy one or an anxious one? Then she opened her eyes. It seemed impossible to imagine such a ride. First of all, Diablo wasn't there, and second, the night was dark, as heavy clouds covered the waning moon.

Sighing, she got back into bed and hoped that she would quickly fall back to sleep. But the fresh air had had a bracing effect on her, and she was more awake than ever.

For about an hour she tried to get back to sleep. When sleep still didn't come, she decided to go down to the kitchen to get a glass of water. It wouldn't make her sleepier, but at least it would quench her thirst.

Carefully, Ricki felt her way down the stairs in the dark and quietly walked toward the kitchen. Strange, had her mother forgotten to turn off the light that evening? The girl opened the kitchen door slowly, so that it wouldn't creak loudly and wake up the rest of the family. She was astounded to find her father in front of the refrigerator.

15

"Hey, Dad, did you wake up hungry?"

Marcus Sulai blushed a little with embarrassment before smiling at his daughter.

"Don't you dare tell your mother on me. She's put me on such a strict diet that my stomach starts rumbling by the middle of the night. If she finds out that I get extra rations secretly she'll be furious with me!"

"Sure." His daughter was very amused. "As far as I'm concerned, you can eat everything in the refrigerator. If you want, I'll even write a confession, so that she thinks it was me."

Marcus sighed with relief.

"That's really nice of you. I owe you one, I promise."

"Honest?" Ricki became totally alert and decided to cash in on this promise before her father could change his mind.

"Honest!" Her father would have promised anything right then. He rummaged inside the fridge and, grabbing bottles, jars, and plastic storage containers, handed them to Ricki, who put them on the table. Within a few minutes he had eaten a few hot dogs, potato salad, loads of pickles, and the bowl of chocolate pudding that was left over from the kids' lunch that afternoon.

"Hmm, that was delicious!" Ricki's father leaned back, satisfied and content, while his daughter got herself a glass of lemonade. She turned the glass around and around in her hand absentmindedly. "There's nothing better than a break-fast after midnight," proclaimed Marcus, but when he got no response from his daughter, he began to observe her carefully.

"Hey, is something wrong? You're so quiet."

Ricki shrugged her shoulders.

"I don't know."

"Hmm…can I help you somehow?" Marcus persisted and moved closer to her.

"It's about this night ride we signed up for," Ricki began hesitantly.

"Oh. And?"

"You know how scared Mom will be if I go along."

"You really can't blame her after all the things that have happened to Diablo in the last few months," interrupted Marcus.

"Yeah, I know, but Mom is always scared when it comes to horses. If she had her way, I probably wouldn't even be allowed to take him out of the paddock." Ricki stared off into the distance.

"It's not that bad," protested Marcus cautiously. "But get to the point."

Ricki was silent for a moment, trying to find the right words.

"You know, I've always tried to understand Mom, but you were there, you heard all the horrible stories she thought up in connection with this night ride. I've always thought that she exaggerates, but today…today Jake said the same kind of things in the stable, and if he said the same things, then —"

"Then that makes you think about it more seriously than when it's only your mother, doesn't it? After all, Jake has had a lot of experience with horses, hasn't he?" Marcus knew immediately what Ricki was trying to explain.

The girl nodded and was silent.

After a while, her father said, "And now you're not so sure that you should go riding with them after all. You're remembering everything that happened and wondering if something similar could happen again."

17

Ricki looked up astonished.

"Exactly. But how did you know?"

Marcus smiled.

"I know you better than you know yourself," he claimed. "So, is *that* your problem?"

Ricki nodded.

"The other kids would laugh at me. On one hand I'm really looking forward to this ride, but on the other hand... I don't know what it is, but all of a sudden, when I was out in the stable this evening, I...I...oh, I just can't explain it."

Ricki's eyes began to water, she was so tired. The young girl tried to hide a yawn behind her hand.

"Go to bed," said Marcus and patted her shoulder lovingly. "If you want, we can talk about it tomorrow, okay? But you need to know one thing: If you have a bad feeling about this night ride, and if you just can't explain this feeling, then maybe you should really think about not going. Usually you can sense when something bad is going to happen." Marcus chuckled so that his words wouldn't seem so serious. "Intuition can be a really good thing, and if you learn to listen to your intuition you can usually save yourself a lot of trouble and pain. But hurry up now and get to bed. It's very late."

Ricki smiled sleepily at her father.

"It's early, Dad! It's three o'clock in the morning!" She got up slowly and awkwardly. "Goodnight...don't get caught!"

"I'll try to get back into bed without being noticed," said Marcus and got up as well.

Ricki was almost out of the kitchen when she turned around once more.

"Dad, is that promise still valid? I mean, that you owe me one?" she asked, leaning against the doorframe.

"Of course, my fellow refrigerator-raiding conspirator!"

"Good. Then I'd like to have gaiters that glow in the dark for Diablo in case I do go on the night ride, and maybe a vest for me that reflects light, so that we can be seen easily in the dark," she blurted out.

Marcus was a little surprised by his daughter's quick response.

"You really got me," he joked and nodded his approval. "I should be glad that your wishes are relatively modest."

"So it's okay?" Ricki asked once more, and Marcus finally pushed her out of the kitchen.

"Yes! This one time! The next time I'll have to be careful what I say."

"Think of your hunger," his daughter warned him, a twinkle in her eye. Then she went back upstairs and to bed.

With a sigh of relief she fell back onto the mattress and was asleep before she had even pulled up the blanket.

Chapter 2

"Hey, Josh is going on the night ride too," announced Lillian the next day when she arrived at the Sulais' stable. Every day she and Cathy and Kevin would meet there to take care of their horses.

"Great!" said Ricki, who was busy trying to comb the knots out of Diablo's thick tail. She was glad for 17-year-old Lillian, a western-style rider who she felt was one of her best friends.

"Hey, do you have any idea if Josh's father has reflecting gaiters and protective glow-in-the-dark vests in his riding shop?" asked Ricki casually.

"I think so. Why do you ask?"

"Well, I promised my father that I would do something really important for him, and he said he would buy me the riding accessories as a thank-you gift," explained Ricki.

"Wow! That's some deal! What did you do that was so important for him?" Kevin wanted to know. His girlfriend smiled broadly.

"I'm keeping his nightly eating binges a secret from Mom! Mom has put him on a diet and the poor guy is starving at night."

Cathy thought that was a hoot.

"Super! And you get riding accessories for that? Tell him that I won't tell anyone either. Maybe I can get a new pair of riding pants out of him! Do you think he would be an easy target?"

"What else do you want, Cathy?"

"Oh, I could think of a few more things – new grooming stuff, maybe a nice saddle cloth for Rashid."

"Okay, you've convinced me," interrupted Ricki. "I think I'll have to talk to Mom and get her to put my poor father back on normal food before he drives our family to the brink of bankruptcy paying off this kind of blackmail in riding accessories."

She put down the comb and gave her black horse a friendly clap on his rump. "So, Diablo, you can move now. Your tail looks like new! You were such a good horse for standing still so long," she praised him extravagantly. Then she began to clean and grease the hooves.

"I think the idea about the gaiters is great," said Kevin. "Are they expensive?"

"Hmm," mulled Ricki. "I think a pair costs about $12."

"Well that's out. I'm as good as broke again," complained Kevin.

"Again? How do you do it? This is the first of the month!" Lillian regarded him with amazement.

"Ever since I got that new CD player from my mom for my birthday, I've been spending a lot of money on CDs. Really good ones, like the boxed sets, are expensive."

"That's true," sighed Cathy. "My last one cost almost $25. It's so lousy that everything costs so much."

Just then, Josh's black-and-white mare, Cherish, stuck her beautiful head in the doorway.

"Hi, you guys!"

Lillian began to sparkle.

"Hey, Cherish, when did you learn to talk?"

In a good mood, Josh took a step inside, leaving his horse on the long lead outside.

"Everything okay here? I thought I'd take advantage of the short break in the rain to let Cherish get a little exercise. By the way, I've already talked with Ziggy today," said the young man. He pulled a folded paper out of his jeans' pocket and handed it to Lillian.

"That's all the information about the night ride: meeting place, time, equipment, rest area, and so on. I hope the gods are favorable to our little outing and send us a really beautiful, warm, rain-free, full-moon night," he laughed.

"Do you all have a good feeling about this night ride?" asked Ricki suddenly.

"Huh? What do you mean?" Kevin stood on tiptoe in order to see over Sharazan's tall back.

"Oh, nothing. Well, do you or don't you?" She repeated her question and got only astonished looks from her friends.

"I haven't thought about it up to now," said Lillian with a wrinkled brow.

"You don't have to think about feelings. Either you have them or you don't. That's what you call intuition," replied Ricki, who was remembering her conversation with her father the previous evening.

"Intuition! That's crazy!" Kevin made a face.

"It's not crazy," Josh intervened. "One time we were sitting around in the riders' clubhouse celebrating someone's birthday, and suddenly I had a funny feeling in the pit of my stomach. I got up and walked into the stable. At first

22

glance, everything seemed to be okay. But then I noticed that Cherish was lying down in her stall and she had colic. One of the little kids who goes into the stable every day had given her way too much old bread that was partially moldy. I even found a slice of it in front of the gate. Luckily I called the vet in time. If I hadn't listened to my intuition, which told me that something wasn't right, my sweet girl might not be alive today."

The teens listened quietly, and even Kevin began to think it over. But before he could say any more about it, Josh was saying his good-byes. He wanted to get home before it started to rain again.

As soon as her boyfriend left, Lillian unfolded the piece of paper and began to read Ziggy's announcement aloud:

Hello, all you brave riders!
Just two more days, and then it's here! Have you all cleaned and groomed your horses and your riding boots? Have you polished your saddles and laid out a raincoat? We're going to ride no matter what the weather is like. The only exception: If there is a thunderstorm or it hails, then we'll stay home. Otherwise we'll meet this coming Friday at 9 p.m. in the parking lot at Echo Lake. You won't need anything but a good mood and, of course, your horses.

On this full-moon night, we will ride around Echo Lake and then over the trails between the Andersons' meadows on to the hunting lodge, where a team of volunteers will be standing by to heat up the grills so that we can have our well-earned break after about two hours of riding. We'll enjoy steaks, hot dogs, and lemonade. Our meal is sponsored by Paul, Sam, and Gus, whom we want to thank in advance on behalf of all of the participants.

About midnight, we'll start off again and ride back the same way to the starting place. From there, you will all find your own way back home. We figure that you'll all be back in your beds by 2 a.m.

In case you're interested, there are 17 riders signed up as of now. Eight of them are young people and—yes, you have counted correctly—9 adult riders. Therefore, kids, your parents don't have to worry; there are enough chaperones on this ride.

Okay, then, see you all on Friday. We're sure that you all will remember this phenomenal ride for a long time to come.

So until then, stay healthy and fit.

Ziggy and Robby

Lillian refolded the letter and placed it on the bench in the stable corridor, then glanced, smiling, at her friends.

"Hey, that sounds great, don't you think? First, riding by full moonlight and then a barbecue...very cool!" She began to get in the mood.

"Full moon on Echo Lake will be fabulous," agreed Cathy.

"And if the old swamp witches sing at midnight, we'll –" Kevin began in a weird, creepy voice.

Lillian cut him off, laughing. "We'll be at the lodge filling our bellies, you big sorcerer!"

Ricki picked up the letter from the bench and read it through again very slowly to herself.

It really sounded great, the way they had planned the ride for Friday night.

Hmm, thought Ricki. *Since most of the riders are going to be adults, how can anything go wrong?*

24

"Oh, whatever," she said all of a sudden. "We've been waiting for just such a ride for a long time, and dreamed about what it would be like to ride in the moonlight. I'm going to assume that nothing bad will happen, and that it will be just as great as Ziggy and Robby say it will be!"

"Super attitude! Finally, you're the same old Ricki!" grinned Kevin.

"I really had the impression that you were going to send us off on our own on Friday," admitted Cathy, and beamed at Ricki happily.

"It would be unrealistic if we expected to do this without any problems," Lillian joined in.

Ricki nodded.

"You're right. Practically speaking, nothing can happen. But right after that accident with Diablo, I'd really thought that I...oh, forget it. Of course I'll go riding with you all!"

Ricki's voice sounded happy and convinced, but deep down she still had some doubts about whether going on this ride was a good idea.

She tried to drown out these negative thoughts before they could take hold, but she wasn't able to do so.

"Look, it's raining cats and dogs again," shouted Cathy.

"I hope Josh made it home before it started," worried Lillian.

"Your Josh isn't made of cotton candy. A little rain isn't going to melt him," Kevin said.

"*Little?* That's an understatement! I'm just glad that I'm dry. Can you imagine riding at night in this weather? If it pours like this on Friday, I'm staying home," decided Cathy. "I think even Rashid wouldn't feel like riding when it's so wet outside."

"Not just Rashid," Ricki agreed. She kept staring out the

window; it was so gray and foggy that she couldn't even see the paddock.

What's wrong with me? she continued to wonder, determined to take up her father's offer and talk with him again this evening. Maybe afterward she'd have a better understanding of her inner doubts and indecision.

*

"Of course, we should also consider that your mother's fears are being dealt with in your subconscious. After all, she's been talking about the ride ever since you brought it up, and has told you about all the things that could happen," said Marcus, putting a wet plate in the dish rack. As he washed and Ricki dried the dinner dishes, he tried to help his daughter understand her vague feeling that something was wrong.

"It could be, but I don't think so," Ricki answered after thinking it over. "Mom's often said stuff, and I never made a crisis out of it before."

"Well, then, there could be another possibility," Marcus said slowly and seriously, looking directly into his daughter's eyes as he handed her the frying pan.

"And that would be?"

"I don't know if I –"

Impatience showed on Ricki's face. "Come on, Dad, I'm not a little kid anymore! I'm going to be 14 soon! Whatever it is, tell me!" She put the dry pan away in the cupboard.

"Let's sit down," Marcus said, motioning Ricki to the table.

"Have I ever told you about your great-grandmother

Clara? She had something that people used to call 'second sight.'"

"What?" Ricki hadn't quite understood him.

"Second sight. It means that a person has some premonitions about certain situations that later actually happen."

"Wow! That's wild!" Ricki found what her father was telling her really interesting.

"Well, anyway, it depends on how you feel about it. Your great-grandmother was one of those people. My mother, your grandmother, told me a lot about her and I even have some memories of her. She could predict bad weather, earthquakes, even volcanic eruptions, exactly to the day, and she always knew in advance if someone in the family was going to have an accident or become ill."

Ricky grinned. "You're kidding me, right?"

Marcus slowly shook his head.

"No. I'm serious about what I'm telling you, and I wouldn't have said anything if you hadn't started it with your persistent 'funny feelings,' which you can't explain."

Looking a little pale, she stared at Marcus uncertainly. Is it possible to know things in advance?

"Are there a lot of people like that?" she asked. "And isn't it a huge burden to know everything that's going to happen in advance? I would hate it if I knew about accidents and stuff like that before they happened."

"You know, there are probably a great many people with this kind of talent, but a lot of them don't talk about it because, first of all, they don't want other people to think they're crazy, and secondly, they don't want to worry the people around them." Ricki's father smiled encouragingly at his daughter.

"But don't worry too much about it. If you have this gift,

27

you'll find out about it soon enough, and if you don't, that's fine too," he said, patting her hand. "I just want to tell you one more thing. It's not always the worst thing to be able to see into the future. Your great-grandmother could prevent many accidents from happening in the first place. She could warn people and make them more cautious about dangerous situations."

Marcus paused, letting Ricki absorb the information. Then he continued. "Grandma Clara also predicted many wonderful things, by the way. For example, my marriage to your mother and the recuperation of my father, who had a very serious lung disease. See, it has its good side too."

Slowly Ricki began to understand.

"And you think…that…that I may—?" She asked softly.

"I don't know, Ricki, but anything's possible. I just hope that I haven't scared you."

"I CERTAINLY HOPE SO, TOO!" Brigitte Sulai had entered the kitchen unexpectedly and, having overheard some of their conversation, was upset about what Marcus had just told their daughter.

"What is wrong with you?!" she chastised her husband. "How can you tell a child things like that? Such a lot of nonsense, and it can be such a burden. Now Ricki won't be able to sleep." Brigitte was really worked up. She shook her head back and forth very agitatedly.

"Brigitte, I know that you never believed in my grand-mother's gift. But you experienced it yourself, and that thing that—"

"Be quiet! I don't want to hear anything more about it!" Brigitte's eyes were shining with alarm. "Ricki, there is no truth to these stories! None! Do you understand?"

"I'm not an idiot," the girl mumbled, rising from her

chair and hurrying past her parents and out of the room. She didn't feel like being a part of this conversation any longer.

Bewildered by the opposite positions of her parents, she decided to go over to the stable. Maybe she'd be able to sort out her thoughts there in peace.

*

The next morning the sun shone brightly, as if to make up for all the rainy days of the past week.

Ricki had slept like a log, and awoke very early.

She got up quickly, sprang to the window, and opened it as far as it would go. She leaned on the windowsill with her elbows and surveyed the surrounding meadows and fields with glowing eyes.

What a beautiful place this is, she thought each time she looked at it. She was so glad her family had moved here and not somewhere else.

Automatically she turned her head toward the stable, where she could already hear the clatter of the manure fork.

Jake is up early today, too, she noticed and hurried into her jeans. She was anxious to go outside and feel the sun on her skin, something she had missed so much in the last few days.

"Good morning, Jake," she called cheerfully from a distance as she approached the stable. "Did you sleep well?"

"Humph," grumbled the old man as he trudged past Ricki.

"Hello, did I say something wrong?" The girl looked after him bewildered. But Jake paid no attention to her.

29

Shrugging her shoulders, Ricki turned and entered the stable, going directly to Diablo. "Hey, good morning, sweetie. Did you, at least, sleep well? I—"

"Did you see the paddock? Everything is muddy and wet!" Jake had returned and was obviously in a bad mood. "The weather is perfect, but the horses have to stay in the stable!"

Ricki looked at him with the same frustration he felt.

"Yes. What a mess. But I think that Lillian and the others will be here by 9 a.m., and then we'll go for a long ride so that the horses can get enough exercise. I just hope it won't be too hot by then," she said, but Jake wasn't in the mood for conversation. He was mad—and when he was mad, Ricki had learned, it was best to stay out of his way.

As quietly as possible the girl hurried to the tack room to get her grooming kit. This morning she had decided to groom all the animals, starting with Diablo so she and her friend wouldn't lose any time later on and could saddle their horses immediately.

She opened Diablo's stall and pulled him out onto the corridor.

"Well, let's get started," she said and got busy.

While she groomed the animals, she thought about the conversation she'd had with her father last evening. In retrospect, it didn't seem as sinister as it had the day before.

Actually, it's pretty cool, she thought, grinning to herself. *I wish I could have gotten to know Great-Grandma Clara.*

*

Two hours later, Lillian, Cathy, and Kevin arrived at the stable with loud greetings.

Ricki grinned.

"I thought this fabulous weather would get you guys out of bed. How about it? Want to go riding?" she asked anxiously.

"Of course!"

"Naturally!"

"That's why we're here."

"Great. We can leave right away. I've already groomed the horses," explained Ricki, carrying her saddle.

"Hey, that's terrific! How long have you been up?" Lillian looked admiringly at her Holli. "Wow, was he clean for once or did you have to work on him with a sponge?"

"Sponge," answered Ricki briefly. "I've been up since 6:30 a.m. The weather is amazing. Hurry up so we can get going."

The kids hurried to saddle their horses, and after they had checked the hooves again the four friends were on their way.

As they were slowly riding away from the farm, Ricki noticed her brother, Harry, running toward the stable.

Ricki halted Diablo for a moment. "What are you doing here so early? You're usually still asleep at this time."

"I want to go for a walk with Chico," answered Harry on the run.

"But don't try to ride him, do you hear me?" his big sister warned. She was relieved when he nodded.

"We're all set!"

The little boy disappeared into the stable, and Ricki brought Diablo back into a trot.

She quickly caught up with the others, and with an exuberant cry, the four rode toward the woods.

"I think I'll have to take a nap tomorrow so that I can be awake for the night ride," said Cathy just as she saw the glistening surface of Echo Lake in the distance.

31

"If you take a nap in the afternoon, I'm sure you won't wake up in time to take part in the ride," joked Kevin.

"If we don't have a little gallop, I'm going to fall asleep right here," yawned Lillian, who usually slept late.

"Then let's go!"

Kevin, who was in the lead, glanced over his shoulder to be sure none of the girls were holding the reins too loosely, and after all three had nodded at him, he pressed his calves into Sharazan's body and let the roan gallop.

Since the trail they were on was fairly narrow, just to be safe, they galloped single file and didn't pass each other.

Contrary to her usual habit, Ricki held the reins tightly, keeping Diablo from running at full gallop.

The black horse shook his head in disapproval. He wanted to run, race, and expend the excess energy that had built up over the last few days of standing around in the stalls, but Ricki kept him under control.

"Hey, are you sleeping? Why don't you let him run a little faster? This trail is perfect!" Cathy could hardly hold back Rashid, who was right behind Diablo.

"Ricki, what's going on? Holli is at his best, for once! Step on it!" Like the others, Lillian couldn't understand why Ricki wasn't riding faster.

"Slowly, boy! Slowly," said Ricki, while she stroked her horse across the neck to comfort him. Ahead of her she observed Kevin on Sharazan, and he was galloping unbelievably fast. Too fast.

Suddenly Ricki screamed.

"KEVIN! WATCH OUT! THE TREE!" She halted Diablo quickly, and Rashid and Holli, not expecting such an abrupt stop from Diablo, nearly collided.

"Ricki, are you crazy?!"

"KEV-VINN! STOP!" Ricki screamed her lungs out but her boyfriend didn't hear her. He allowed Sharazan to continue galloping, without a care in the world.

"The tree…it's going to fall over," whispered Ricki, as pale as a ghost.

"What tree? What are you talking about?" Lillian stared at her friend completely bewildered, as Ricki just pointed in front of them.

Kevin heard a loud bang behind him and looked back even before he reined in Sharazan.

Oh, God, that's unbelievable, he thought desperately. He brought his horse to a standstill and then turned him around.

Coming onto the trail was a burly man wearing a hard hat and heavy work gloves. "Hey kid, are you crazy? Didn't you see the sign we put up at the beginning of the trail? We're felling a few trees here! You were really lucky that you weren't five seconds earlier." The man's voice sounded both furious and also relieved.

Only then did Ricki's boyfriend understand the situation and what a close call he had. His knees began to tremble as he saw the huge evergreen lying across the trail in front of him. His bones felt like rubber and all the color had drained out of his face.

"I…I…really didn't see anything," he stammered. He felt as though he was about to fall off his horse any second. "Wow, all of a sudden I feel sick to my stomach. I think I'm going to—"

"Kevin . . . Kevin! Are you all right?" Ricki's worried shouts could be heard behind the downed evergreen as the girls came riding up.

"Everything's okay, girls. Nothing happened to your

friend. He was really lucky," shouted the logger, standing in the middle of the trail.

Very slowly, Kevin rode around the evergreen, and Ricki was shocked to see his pale face.

"There must have been a sign," he said. His voice was still a little shaky. "Did you guys see it?"

The girls looked at one another and slowly shook their heads no.

"Whatever," said the logger. "The best thing would be for you to ride back home. We have to keep working here or we won't get done today," the man said, and smiled encouragingly at the four. "And please, be more careful about where you're riding. We don't want anything else to happen."

Still in shock, the kids said good-bye and started back home, all of them unusually quiet. Soon they could hear the sounds of a power saw. The shrill sound, as the saw ate into a tree trunk, went right through them and gave them goose bumps.

"Didn't you hear me shouting?" Ricki asked the boy, who was still sitting on Sharazan as though he were drugged.

Kevin shook his head no. Still reeling from the shock, he didn't notice when Lillian suddenly turned to Ricki and asked, "Say, how did you know that a tree was being felled? We didn't see anyone and we didn't see any signs, and the tree wasn't moving…nothing. Can you see into the future?"

Ricki jumped. She remembered what her father had told her about her great-grandmother Clara.

"I have no idea! It was just there all of a sudden." The girl tried to find an answer. "I just knew somehow. That's why I screamed and that's why I wasn't galloping any faster. Strange."

"That really is spooky," commented Cathy, and pointed at a triangular sign that was right by the side of the trail. "I think that somehow you actually saw the sign but didn't realize it until later. I don't really believe in crystal balls," she laughed and added, "You're much too grounded to be able to float and see into the future."

Lillian laughed too, and even Kevin, who was beginning to recover from his near-miss, tried to smile. Ricki was the only one who didn't feel like smiling.

I wonder if I got this gift from Clara? she asked herself silently. But then she decided to believe what Cathy had said about the sign. That explanation appealed to her much more than the idea of seeing into the future like Clara.

I'll be glad when we're home again, she thought. As they rode back, she kept stealing glances at Kevin. He seemed to have recovered fully and regained his sense of humor. He was joking with Lillian and Cathy.

"I'm so glad that nothing happened to you," she told him a while later, and gave him an affectionate smile.

"Me too," grinned Kevin. "How else could I have gone on the ride tomorrow with everyone?"

Oh, God! Tomorrow! I'd completely forgotten, thought Ricki, as a worried look returned to her face. More than ever, after today's experience, she had a bad feeling about tomorrow.

Chapter 3

The gods, it seemed, were smiling on the young riders. The morning promised beautiful weather all day.

As was her custom, Ricki got to the stable early in order to greet Diablo and his stable mates.

Afterward, as she helped Jake with his work in the stalls, she noticed he was in a better mood than he'd been the day before.

"I guess I'll have to get used to doing the stalls alone when your summer vacation is over," he said, putting down fresh hay. Ricki made a face as though she was sucking on a lemon.

"Do you have to remind me on such a beautiful day that the stress will soon start up again? Classes, tests, homework, studying. Life would be so wonderful if school didn't exist."

Jake shook his head disapprovingly. "I hope you won't forget the promise you made when you received Diablo from—"

Ricki laughed. "Oh, Jake, how could I forget that? Diablo reminds me every day. No, no, don't worry. I'm really going to try to bring home decent grades."

"And what stops you from trying to get not just decent grades but really good grades?" asked Jake. "If you're trying to achieve something, set your goal higher than you think you can reach. You'll see you can achieve anything if you set your mind to it and then really work for it, but you won't get something for nothing. Do you understand that?"

Ricki nodded and sighed.

"Yeah, Jake, you've preached that to me about a hundred times already. I understand."

The old stable master grinned.

"You can't repeat something like that too often."

With a glance at Diablo, he changed the subject and asked, "Have you decided whether or not you're going to go on the midnight ride tonight?"

Ricki shrugged her shoulders.

"I don't know. Probably. Oh, I just don't know what I should do. I've been looking forward to this ride for days, but the closer it gets, the less sure I am about it."

"So," the old man replied, "are you afraid that something could happen to Diablo, and that's why you can't make up your mind?"

Ricki hesitated before answering. She tried to hear her inner voice in order to answer the question honestly, but neither yes nor no seemed to pop into her head.

"I don't think that's the reason." She was thinking out loud. "After all, I've been out riding several times since Diablo's accident, and I know that he's a very surefooted trail horse. I can't explain it. Say, Jake, do you believe in clairvoyance?"

The stableman put down the pitchfork and turned around.

"What?"

"Clairvoyance!" repeated Ricki, staring at the old man anxiously.

"Nonsense!" he replied, without even thinking about it. "Humbug, deception, tricks, just hocus-pocus and tomfoolery! Why are you asking me about something like that all of a sudden?"

"Oh, no reason. Let's forget about it, okay? It's not important!" Ricki just waved him off and turned aside to avoid Jake's penetrating gaze.

"I think I'll just go back to the house," she said casually. "Cathy was going to call." She broke off and quickly left the stable.

Jake watched her go, shaking his head.

"Clairvoyance! It's unbelievable, the stuff kids think about these days!"

*

The four teenagers spent a lazy afternoon partly in the stable and partly on the Sulais' porch. It was so hot that even the slightest movement seemed too strenuous.

"I could just go to sleep," complained Lillian, while trying to get comfortable on one of the deck chairs. In no time, she dozed off.

"Me, too," Cathy admitted. "And the idea that I won't get to bed until 2 a.m. doesn't exactly make me want to celebrate!"

"You guys are really a bunch of wimps!" Kevin grinned. "If you keep going on like this, I'll be the only one riding tonight." Nothing in the world would have made him admit to the girls that the heat and weariness were bothering him too.

*

After what seemed like an eternity, it was finally 8 p.m., and the friends were preparing their horses for the evening ride and checking their saddle equipment to make sure there were no defects.

"Everything's fine," said Ricki, who had tested and retested each buckle and every single strap on the saddle as well as the snaffle.

That afternoon she'd decided, once and for all, to take part in the midnight ride.

"Whatever happens," she joked with Lillian, "it can't be as bad as my imagination."

"Nothing will happen!" her girlfriend reassured her. "Remember: When angels ride, nothing bad happens!"

"People! I'm really excited!" Cathy couldn't stand still, and kept pacing and looking at the clock on the wall of the tack room. "I've been watching the clock for at least a half an hour, and the hands don't seem to move! Ricki, is there even a battery in it?"

"Of course, I changed the battery yesterday."

"It must be an old one!" Cathy complained.

"Man, don't be so nervous! You're impossible to put up with," groaned Kevin.

"How long are we going to wait before we start off?" the girl wanted to know.

"I'd say if we leave at 8:30 p.m., we should be at the meeting place exactly on time," Lillian answered, as she sat in front of Holli rubbing grease onto his hooves.

"Oh, God, still so long... Well, waiting just isn't my thing," admitted Cathy.

"Haven't you ever noticed that life in general is just a matter of waiting?" asked Kevin. But the girl was concentrating so hard on the clock that she didn't really hear him.

*

"Finally," Cathy sighed in relief as Lillian, about 20 minutes later, gave the signal to saddle up.

Ricki put the new gaiters on Diablo and pulled on the reflecting vest. She had bought the accessories, with her father's help, the day before, after returning from the unsettling ride in the woods.

"Are you guys ready?" Kevin called from Sharazan's stall. A chorus of three answered, "Yeah!"

"Well, then, let's go!"

Brigitte and Jake had just come out the front door of the house as the four friends were mounting up in the courtyard.

"Hey, have fun, and be careful. Ricki, do you have your flashlight? And do you have an extra sweatshirt with you? It can get pretty cold in the middle of the night. And—"

"Everything's all set, Mom. Don't worry. I've got everything I need," Ricki, already mounted on Diablo, shouted across the yard. Far enough away from Brigitte that her mother couldn't hear her, she looked up at the sky, rolled her eyes, and groaned softly, "Jeepers, let's get going before she gets me a winter coat, a halogen floodlight, and possibly a seat belt!"

Kevin and the girls grinned at her and, turning their horses onto the driveway, started for the road.

"But…"

"Bye, Mrs. Sulai! See you, Jake!" the others called out in unison. "We've got to get going, or the group might leave without us."

"Thanks." Ricki breathed a sigh of relief, and the four friends finally rode off.

Brigitte stood in front of the house for quite a while, watching them ride into the distance. "If only they come back safely," she said softly.

Jake touched her arm reassuringly. "Nothing will happen to them. The only thing that will hurt Ricki when she comes home will be her backside. The new saddle hasn't been broken in yet."

*

The kids rode on, holding their reins loosely. The horses, glad to be out of their stalls, were enjoying the exercise and seemed to be more fit than ever.

"No wonder, they dozed in their stalls all day," commented Cathy.

"Instead of talking all afternoon, we should have taken a nap. The heat really gets to you, don't you think?" Ricki felt pretty tired.

"Well, I slept for a while, but it didn't help much," Lillian replied. Kevin seemed to be the only one who felt really good.

"You can still turn back," he said, grinning. "Mama Sulai would be happy if her little girl were home in bed instead of riding through the night."

Ricki stuck her tongue out at him.

"Too late," she laughed at him. To be honest, the evening was beginning to be fun for her. The troubling thoughts she'd had before the ride had been replaced by excitement and curiosity.

The kids rode at the edge of the field in single file. After an initial period of noisy joking and laughter, their mood changed to one of peace and tranquility. They sat silently on their horses and enjoyed the calm that dusk brings at the day's end. Here and there the friends saw rabbits, which sprang back and forth over the trail in giant hops. They even spied a fox. He crouched down and waited until the horses were about thirty feet away. Then the bushy-tailed animal ran away.

"Look up there, at the edge of the woods. Can you see the deer?" Ricki called softly to her friends.

They stopped their horses for a moment in order to take in the idyllic picture.

"Beautiful," whispered Lillian, so that the shy animals wouldn't be frightened away. "They're standing there so peacefully in the evening light."

Cathy nodded in agreement. She loved these delicate creatures, which, unfortunately, always took off when anyone came near them.

"We've got to get going," warned Kevin, "otherwise they really will start without us."

"Too bad," joined in Ricki. As the horses started to move again, the heads of the deer jolted up, and in less than ten seconds they disappeared into the woods.

*

Soon the four friends were nearing the parking lot at Echo Lake. Several small spots of light, probably from flashlights, were visible in the distance, and headlights from the cars lit up the parking lot as well. Many of the adult riders had decided to transport their horses in trailers to the start of the ride. They needed the light from the cars while they unloaded their animals, so that the horses wouldn't take a false step going down the ramps.

"Hello! Wow, you guys are right on time! To the minute! Did you take a test ride in the last few days to see how long it would take you to ride here? Great to see you!" Ziggy came over to the four, who had just arrived, leading his gelding, Halifax. Robby, who was handing out safety reflectors to everyone, waved at them.

"Please attach them to both sides of your boots. If anyone comes upon us, or a car happens to be on the road where we are riding, he'll be able to see us from a distance," Robby explained.

Ziggy took in Ricki's new gear. "Man, Ricki, you're wearing a real professional outfit. Reflecting gaiters, safety vest—that should be enough to prevent anything from happening," he laughed.

"So, everyone, everything all set?" asked Robby about ten minutes later. After general agreement, he shouted happily, "Well, then, saddle up and let's get under way!"

Quickly he got the riders into line, and he made sure that the young riders were placed among experienced riders so that the adults could watch out for them.

Robby was at the front, while Ziggy went to the end of the line. Each man wore a light on his belt that served to mark the beginning and the end of the chain of riders. With the blinking red safety lights that all the riders had on their boots the group looked like a giant centipede.

Josh, who had arrived at the parking lot at the last minute, moved his Cherish into position behind Lillian and her Doc Holliday.

"Are you excited?" he asked.

"Not really," his girlfriend answered casually. But she looked back over her shoulder and asked herself if there was anyone there, with the exception of Ziggy and Robby, of course, whose heart wasn't beating faster than usual. After all, this was the first night ride for most of the participants.

*

"Oh, look how beautifully the moon is reflected on the lake," Ricki raved. "Like thousands—no—like millions of points of light dancing on the surface of the water."

The girl was enraptured by the beauty of the scene. In her imagination she heard an ethereal melody and saw elves and fairies floating hand in hand across the lake like dragonflies, playing in the magic of the moonlight.

Ricki was a dreamer, and she always found it wonderful to enter into a world of fantasy and suddenly see things in herself and around her that existed only in her own thoughts; it was a world that never failed to enchant her.

Diablo carried her carefully over the narrow trails and swayed her gently into her dream world, where she was alone with her horse and totally at peace. The conversations and the laughter of the other riders and the picture of the entire group began to dissolve, and she imagined herself alone, riding Diablo bareback along the banks of the lake. She saw herself as a being of nature, all lightness and ease, spreading harmony and joy throughout the world. Just one motion with her silky wings would be enough to transform the spots of light on the surface of the water into a glistening sea of stars, full of love and peace, which rose upward to cover the entire planet. Diablo, her loyal companion, would carry her everywhere the light of love was needed in the shadowy places of the world.

Ricki sighed softly and immersed herself in this fantasy for quite a while.

"Hey, Ricki! Ric-ki! What's happening with you? Have you gone to sleep?" someone called behind her, and her dream of a peaceful world burst like a soap bubble.

"Hey, I think she's really sleeping!" She heard Kevin's voice again.

"No way," she replied. "I was just thinking about something."

Lovingly, she stroked her black horse's neck and played with his mane. She was sure that he had experienced her dream, just as she did.

"They would never understand it," Ricki said softly to Diablo. She had to look around a bit to figure out where they were. She'd been so lost in her thoughts that she hadn't been paying attention to the trail, but Diablo was always reliable. The trust that Ricki had in her horse was worth more than the greatest treasures in the world.

Robby left the path that went around Echo Lake and went down a meadow path that was as familiar to the four friends as their own rooms.

The light on Robby's belt beamed out over the ears of his horse, making a ghostly silhouette of the horse's head.

Now that the riders had left the woods, the surrounding area was vaguely visible in the moonlight. The horses were more sure of their steps now that they could see where they were going.

"Wow, I would really have missed something if I hadn't come along," Ricki admitted. There was something very special about horseback riding at night.

"See, nothing happened," grinned Kevin.

Off in the distance, the glare of the barbecue fire, which had been started by some of Robby's friends, became visible.

"We aren't home yet," countered Ricki. She was annoyed that her boyfriend was reminding her of her worrisome feelings over the last few days.

Hearing the exchange between the couple, Cathy exclaimed, "Oh, you old worrywart, are you going to start that again? Can't you just enjoy the ride and assume that everything's going to be just fine? It's not like you at all!"

That's easy for you to say, thought Ricki. *If you knew about Clara, you might think differently about my weird premonitions.*

"Ricki, what's going on with you? Have you become one of those oracles who predict bad news?" Lillian turned around in her saddle, looked past Josh, and smiled at her friend.

I've got to talk to them, but not now, not on this ride, or I'll ruin it for them, Ricki thought as she glanced up at the sky.

Dark cloud formations were moving toward the moon, so that it was only a question of time before the night would be as dark as a moonless night.

"Hey, people, can you smell the hot dogs and the steaks? Link and Susanna timed it just right for when we arrive at the barbecue pit." Ziggy licked his lips in anticipation, and the other riders began to be excited, too. Their mouths were watering at the thought of the pre-midnight meal that had been prepared for them.

Most of the riders fell silent, staring at the fire and thinking about the culinary pleasures awaiting them at the lodge, while their animals plodded on unimpressed.

"A fire like that has something mystical about it," pronounced Kevin as they drew near to the night's rest area.

"That's true…as long as it's under control," responded Ricki, and before Kevin could even answer her, she said quickly: "I know what you're about to say, but I was just thinking about the fire at the riding academy!"

"Hmm, you're right. I was afraid you were going to spoil the barbecue by predicting something about the fire."

Ricki decided to say no more about it.

A short distance from the campfire, the riders stopped their horses, all of whom were staring at the fire with huge eyes. Once in a while a nervous snorting was heard, but soon the horses quieted down.

Susanna and Link had prepared everything perfectly. The young woman had transported a few picnic tables to the spot in her beat-up old VW camper, and they had been placed far enough away from the fire, so that the riders could sit down and still keep hold of the reins.

"Hey!" shouted Link, waving a greeting with the huge barbecue fork he was using to turn the hot dogs and steaks on the grill. "How was the ride so far? You arrived just in time. The first steaks are just about done to perfection!"

Susanna laughed with the other riders. "I made a huge container of potato salad. Paper plates and tableware are back there in the box." She pointed to the first picnic table.

"Wow, you two are really great," Albert Perkins praised them. He had come along on the ride with his wife, Lisa. It was a miracle he was so positive. Usually he was a complainer. He swung down from his mare, undid the saddle belt, and handed his wife the reins.

"I'll go and get us some food!" he said and started off toward the barbecue pit. "Two portions of steak and potato salad, please," he requested.

"Two plates, please!" grinned Susanna, holding out her hands.

"What?"

47

"Plates!"

"Oh, yeah, of course. Lisa, could you?"

"No, not unless you hold the reins," she replied.

Albert Perkins made a sour face. If he left the front of the food line now, he would have to wait a while before the second group of steaks was ready. Behind him, the riders were already waiting their turns.

"Then just two steaks without potato salad, in rolls," he grumbled somewhat angrily, but Susanna wouldn't allow him to ruin her good mood.

"You'll still need plates, Mr. Perkins. We believe in first come, first served, but there is plenty for everyone."

"That Perkins thinks he's getting shortchanged," the chubby man heard someone behind him whisper. "Just like at the shows. If he doesn't win a ribbon, he will even go so far as to blame the judges!"

Albert Perkins turned around brusquely, but all he could see were innocent-looking faces.

"That's outrageous! It's simply slanderous! I'm going to—"

"Come on, Albert. Others are hungry, too!" yelled Ziggy, who was standing way back in the line waving his paper plate.

"Why did I let Lisa talk me into going on this night ride?" Perkins, now in a really bad mood, grumbled to himself.

Just then his wife handed him two plates. Sensing her husband was about to make a scene, Lisa had handed their horses over to another rider and gone to get the dinnerware herself.

Albert Perkins observed the steaks that Susanna put onto his plate with the eye of a gourmet chef.

"They were on the grill much too long," he complained. "They look so black! They're going to be as tough as leather."

"Black as night, Mr. Perkins! I hope they taste good, enjoy!" Link had already taken Kevin's plate, so the man couldn't do anything but move forward and give him some space.

While Albert Perkins was morosely stomping his way over to the tables, Kevin said, "When he doesn't have anything to complain about, he's just not happy. I'm surprised that he even came along."

"I wonder if he's like that at home, always complaining." Ricki said. She was right behind Kevin in line. "I feel sorry for his wife."

"Lisa? Yeah, she's so nice, I don't know how she puts up with him!"

"Next, please." Link held Kevin's full plate out to him, and the boy stepped aside.

Cathy, behind Ricki, grinned. "Ow, that reminds me of the dentist," she said, as Ricki now took her steak as well.

"According to Perkins, we'll need a dentist if we eat this meat," she laughed.

Together, the three walked back to Lillian, who had been holding the horses.

"Here, Lily, a special steak designed to test the strength of your teeth!" Cathy handed the platter to her friend.

"Oh, thanks. I've been looking forward to this all day. Deee-licious!"

The young friends had retrieved their horses and sat on the ground a little bit away from the tables, where most of the adults were sitting.

"I don't think it's right that they've allowed children to

come along on this ride. Nowadays, kids don't have any sense of responsibility. They don't know how to behave when an emergency arises. Then we adults, with our experience, have to take care of that lot, to make sure they get back home safely."

They all could hear the loud voice of Albert Perkins.

"Now, Albert, there weren't any emergencies, and anyway, I think when the young people with their own horses—" Lisa tried to calm her husband, but the old grump just silenced her with a gesture.

"Oh, nonsense! Did you see how… ?"

"He's apparently forgotten that there are plenty of adults who have no sense of responsibility," Ricki said angrily. "Why else are there wars?"

"Come on, Ricki, don't let him upset you. That Perkins is just an old grouch. Let's not let him ruin our whole evening," intervened Cathy, and Lillian nodded in agreement.

In between bites, Lillian said, "Evening? It's the middle of the night, in case you haven't noticed."

Ricki strained her eyes in order to see the time on her wristwatch.

"Hey, it's after 11. It's unbelievable how quickly time flies. In another 45 minutes we'll be on our way again," she said, and then she handed Diablo's reins to Kevin.

"I need to get something to drink. Anybody else?" Ricki asked.

"No thanks," said Lillian, and the others shook their heads no as well.

"Okay, see you later." Ricki ran around the tables to get to Susanna's camper. Coolers of various beverages were piled in front of it.

It's really dark, in spite of there being a full moon, she

50

thought. She had to pay attention so that she got the cola she wanted and not something else.

As she pulled the metal tab and held the can up to her lips, she felt a light breeze on her hair. Ricki looked up and realized that the full moon was now almost completely covered by clouds.

"Oh no," the girl exclaimed, and hurried back to her friends.

"There's a storm coming," she called to them and pointed toward the sky. "I don't think we'd better wait too long before we get going."

"Oh, it won't start for a while," commented Robby, who had heard Ricki shout.

"I wouldn't bet on it," answered Ricki, and took Diablo's reins back from Cathy.

The black horse had raised his head and breathed in the air through his nostrils. His ears moved about nervously, and Ricki noticed that the pupils of his eyes had widened. She looked around and noticed that Diablo wasn't the only horse that had become restless.

"Something's wrong…we should go back," she said emphatically.

"Girls that are afraid of the dark shouldn't participate in moonlight rides," commented Albert Perkins nastily. He clapped his right hand loudly against his thigh and said: "I don't feel like being your baby-sitter later on!"

Ricki looked over at him.

"I'm not afraid, Mr. Perkins, but look at the sky, and the horses, too! They're getting restless, and that means—"

"Oh, we have a lady horse whisperer among us! Little girl, in two and a half hours, you'll be back in your little bed and then you can get your mama to comfort you!"

"What a stupid jerk!" Ricki said softly under her breath as she tried to calm Diablo by stroking his neck. "It's okay, my darling, don't be afraid. Everything's all right."

"Maybe you should have gotten a little kitten instead of a horse!" Albert Perkins couldn't stop.

"That's enough, Mr. Perkins!" Kevin stood in front of Ricki and glared at the man. What right did he have to make fun of his girlfriend like that?

"Ooh," Perkins jeered. "Mister Guardian Angel is here, too."

"Albert, please." Lisa looked around helplessly. She was so ashamed of the things her husband had just said. "Don't you want to drink something besides beer?" she asked him quietly, just as he was opening a new bottle.

"Mind your own business!" Albert Perkins never let anyone criticize him, especially his wife.

"Let it be, Kevin," intervened Ricki. She was focused entirely on Diablo, who was becoming increasingly more agitated. He shook his beautiful head desperately and began to scrape the ground wildly with his hooves.

"Calm down, Diablo. It'll be okay. I know, something's wrong, but we have to wait until the others have figured it out, too," she explained to her horse. The black horse, however, didn't seem to want to wait. He whinnied shrilly and then stood entirely still and puffed out his nostrils.

Chapter 4

"Holli's beginning to act a little weird, too," Lillian exclaimed. "I think you're right. We should start to head for
home very soon."

"Now *she's* acting up," Perkins sneered out loud. "What
a kindergarten I'm in the middle of!"

Ziggy and Robby were standing together near the picnic
tables. Although they had joined in the laughter when
Albert Perkins first began to tease Ricki, they now looked
up apprehensively at the sky, which seemed to grow darker
and darker as more clouds rolled in to block the moonlight.

The breeze had picked up and sent napkins and paper
plates flying off the tables. The riders hurriedly collected
their used plates and utensils and put them into a garbage
bag so they wouldn't be blown away, and then went around
gathering up those on the ground.

"What do you think?" Ziggy turned to Robby and asked.
"Maybe Ricki's right. If the wind keeps getting stronger,
the weather could change suddenly, and who knows what
could happen."

Robby nodded. "I agree. I don't feel like being out here
in a storm. Let's get going as fast as possible! After all,
we're responsible for getting these kids home safely!"

"People, finish up. We're leaving for home," Ziggy called out. All he got in return were puzzled looks.

"What? But it's not even 11:30 p.m. yet! I thought we agreed to leave at midnight."

"Yeah, that was the plan, but considering the fact that—"

"—that a frightened girl is making the entire crew crazy, we have to go home." Albert Perkins looked around, waiting for general approval, and he actually managed to get one or two of the other adult riders, who were reluctant to leave the free food and drink, to speak out against riding home earlier than planned.

"Ah, c'mon, Ziggy, it was just getting so cozy!"

"If we leave now, all the work that went into it won't have been worth it! Hey, Susanna, are there any more steaks?"

Robby had given Susanna a heads-up, and the young woman responded very casually:

"I'm sorry, but we're all out! We didn't think you'd all be so starved that you'd eat three steaks apiece!"

I guess the organizers didn't plan ahead, did they?" Albert Perkins got up a little awkwardly. "I'm going to get myself another beer!"

"Albert, we're leaving for home. *Now!*" Ziggy blocked the way of the slightly tipsy man.

"Go ahead, go ahead, but I'm going to have another beer!" Perkins tried to push Ziggy out of the way, but the young man stood his ground.

"Albert, I promised the parents of these kids that I would see they got home safely. I planned this ride and have full responsibility, and therefore complete authority. So, under the circumstances, I have decided that we are going back home—and we are leaving immediately!"

"Well, well, our brave and fearless leader has spoken,"

Perkins mocked him. Ziggy's words, however, had brought the other adult riders to their feet, so he shrugged his shoulders and leaned against his horse.

"Wimps," he said thickly, "they're all wimps!"

Ziggy breathed a sigh of relief. While Link hurried to put out the fire, Susanna had already begun to gather up everything so that the two of them could stow it all in the camper.

In the meantime, the riders tightened their saddle girths and then mounted their horses.

"Hold still, Sharazan, hold still. What's wrong with you all of a sudden?" Kevin was having problems mounting his roan. Each time he tried to put his foot in the stirrup, the horse laid his ears back and stepped backward.

"Wait a minute, I'll hold him until you're up," called Cathy, and pulled her horse, Rashid, behind her. She held Sharazan tightly by the reins, but just as Kevin was about to push upward into the saddle, there was a bright flash of lightning, and Rashid panicked and bucked.

Cathy had to make a split-second decision as to whether to let go of Sharazan or Rashid. She felt more responsible for her horse, and so she decided in favor of him.

"Stay calm, Rashid. Stand still. Everything's okay…good boy." She spoke to the horse as softly as possible to comfort him. But she turned around suddenly as she heard Kevin yell.

"What's the matter with you? Sharazan, no!"

Now the other riders were alerted.

"What's going on over there?"

"Who just yelled?"

Ricki and Lillian were already mounted on their horses and were waiting for Ziggy to give the signal to ride.

As Kevin kept yelling, all they could see in the dark was Sharazan bucking like a rodeo horse.

"He's going to bolt!" exclaimed Ricki suddenly, and turned white as a sheet.

"No, he's just stubborn!" replied Lillian, but Ricki just shook her head violently.

"No! He's going to bo—"

"Heeelp! Sharazan! No!" Kevin's scream echoed through the night. When the horse had started bucking, he hadn't yet swung into the saddle. Desperate, he clung to Sharazan's mane. He realized that his foot had slid through the stirrup and was caught while he was still lying across the saddle.

Just don't fall down, Kevin begged in a panic. *I can't get out of this stupid stirrup. . .*

Quick as a flash, Ricki pressed her calves into Diablo's belly, so that now he, too, was frightened and made a leap forward. In two or three gallops he was where Sharazan had stood only seconds earlier.

"Sharazan! Heeelp!" Kevin's voice could be heard again, but by now it was some distance away.

"Oh, man, what are we going to do?" Cathy looked into the night in horror and her entire body trembled. "I just couldn't hold him any longer. Rashid was rearing, and—"

"That doesn't matter! We have to go after him," said Ricki with determination. She was very frightened for her boyfriend, and Ziggy was hardly able to hold her back.

"Stop! We have no idea where Sharazan has run off to, and we can hardly see anything in the dark."

Not too far away the rumble of thunder could be heard, and the wind was getting stronger and stronger.

"Why does it have to storm now? As if we didn't have

enough problems," Lillian complained, and watched Ricki, who had flinched at the word *storm.* In her mind's eye she could still see the burning house after it had been struck by lightning, and this memory had tormented her since childhood. Kevin's screams for help jolted her back into the present.

"We've got to get home. The thunderstorm will be here soon," Albert Perkins could be heard complaining.

"Sorry, Albert, Kevin's horse has bolted and we can't leave without him."

"What do I care about Kevin? If he's as good a rider as he claims to be, he'll get his horse under control soon and then he'll come back."

"That's enough!" Ricki's voice boomed, perhaps a little too shrilly. But she couldn't help it. She was angry with the insensitive man, who was showing signs of drunkenness, and also fearful for Kevin. "If we had started out when I said we should, all of this could have been avoided! I'm going to ride after Kevin right now!"

Robby reached out and grabbed Diablo's reins.

"You're not going to ride anywhere!" he said firmly, and both his look and tone of voice told her not to argue. "If anything should happen to you, too, well, that really would be a mess!"

"Well, then, do something!" Ricki shouted at him.

"We definitely have to wait for him," said Ziggy. He remained so calm that Ricki envied him. Robby, however, shook his head no.

"We can't risk something else happening. I suggest that I wait here for a while, while you take the others back to Echo Lake. If you take the trail along the woods, you should be there in about half an hour."

57

"Good, but you shouldn't wait alone. That's too dangerous."

"I'll stay here with Robby." Josh had just joined the group on Cherish.

"And I'm staying for sure!" Ricki insisted.

"Then I'm staying here, too," said Lillian, but Josh shook his head.

"Oh no! That's all we need! You two are riding back home with the others," he ordered.

"I hope you don't think I'm going anywhere until I know what's happening with Kevin," Ricki protested again.

This time, Josh's voice sounded harsher than even he had intended: "For the last time: *you are riding back with the others!* You won't help Kevin by getting lost yourself! Is that clear?"

Ricki felt her eyes fill with tears, but since the sky was beginning to look really ominous, she gave in and nodded sadly.

"Okay, good. Let's go!" Ziggy gathered all the riders together. "Let's get home as quickly as possible. Robby, I'll come back with the horse transport as soon as I can and pick you up. Make sure that you ride back the same way we came, so that I can't possibly miss you!"

Robby nodded.

"Better get going. The weather isn't going to get any better!" Almost as a confirmation, a loud clap of thunder suddenly cut through the night.

The horses whinnied nervously.

Against her will and with her heart beating wildly, Ricki went to the end of the line of riders. She didn't want to leave Robby and Josh behind without knowing that they were really going to return with Kevin later.

She regarded the heavens full of apprehension. Bolts of lightning flashed one after the other across the sky, trading off with heat flashes that were ghostly quiet. The only advantage was that the lightning illuminated the trail, helping the riders find their way.

Please, no lightning strikes, and please…let Kevin be okay, prayed Ricki to herself. It was all she could do to keep Diablo in line at a slow pace. His nerves were just as taut as hers. She felt she was sitting astride a keg of dynamite.

*

Racing with fear, Sharazan had disappeared into the darkness, and had covered quite a distance in a relatively short time.

Kevin was still weakly hanging on to one side of the saddle. He clutched the mane tightly in one hand, and with the other he grasped the leather. He tried as hard as he could not to slide down completely. He knew he would be lost if he actually fell off. He had read too many reports of riders getting caught in the stirrup and being dragged to death by their horses.

For God's sake, stop! he silently implored Sharazan the whole time. He realized that with every galloping step Sharazan took, his own strength was diminishing. Right from the beginning, Kevin had lost the reins, so he had no chance of controlling Sharazan's speed. How could he? The only thing going through his mind was the fear he wouldn't be able to hang on much longer. If Sharazan didn't stop his gallop soon, he would—but Kevin wouldn't think about it. Gradually he couldn't think straight anymore, anyway.

59

Unhindered, Sharazan galloped on and tried to get rid of the annoying thing hanging on to one side of his body. He didn't seem to realize it was Kevin, whom he loved more than anything else.

Trying to escape the bright violent flashes of lightning that cut across the sky and the terrible noise of the thunder that exceeded the howling of the wind, he raced ahead at breakneck speed, his ears laid back, without knowing what lay beyond him in the darkness.

Kevin struggled valiantly to hang on, but he was growing more tired by the second.

Ricki…he thought, and then he began to lose consciousness.

*

Josh and Robby were still waiting at the lodge's barbecue area with their horses.

"I have a funny feeling that Kevin isn't going to come back here," Lillian's boyfriend said, looking earnestly at Robby. "Maybe we should leave and start looking for him."

"You're kidding, right? To be honest, I'm already nervous when I think about us standing here, a target, in this thunderstorm. I can tell you this, that was the first and the last moonlight ride I organize, let alone participate in! Anyway, where should we look? Sharazan could have gone anywhere."

Josh nodded sadly. Of course he knew it was ridiculous to start looking for Kevin, but it seemed worse just to stand there waiting for a miracle to happen.

"We could take off in the camper and look around," offered Susanna, looking at Link, who nodded in agreement.

"In a thunderstorm it's best to travel in a car, anyway," he said, and tried to smile despite his uneasiness.

"It isn't the worst idea," said Josh. He shined Robby's light onto his watch. "Two minutes past midnight. I suggest we wait here another 15 minutes and, if Kevin doesn't show up, then we'll leave, too. The storm is getting worse and worse, and I have to admit, I'll be glad when Cherish is back safe in her stall."

"Good." Susanna and Link nodded at the two other men. "Have a safe trip back home," the young woman wished them. As they headed to the camper, she turned and added: "I hope we find Kevin and his horse—uninjured."

Josh and Robby watched as the two drove off in the old VW camper.

If only there was more light so that you could see something, thought Josh, and his companion seemed to guess what was on his mind.

"It's the only thing we can do right now," he said.

"What do you mean?"

"Well, have the two of them take off in the camper. If we were all on horseback, we'd have no chance."

*

The storm had grown in intensity, and fierce winds whipped the rain into the faces of the riders. In a very short time they were soaked to the skin and wishing they were finally back at the starting place.

Lillian and Cathy, who were riding in front of Ricki, had pulled their collars up to protect their necks, with their eyes looking down. They were freezing cold. They kept turning around to give their girlfriend encouraging looks, but Ricki

61

didn't seem to notice. She was much too worried about Kevin, who was somewhere out there with Sharazan in the storm alone.

Ricki could still hear his shrill screams for help.

She realized that she'd never heard Kevin scream before. What had made him do it?

She hated to think what might have happened by now.

If only Sharazan hadn't taken a false step in the darkness, thought Ricki. *And if only Kevin hasn't fallen off... If only he was on his way back.*

Ricki was sick with worry. She stared at Diablo's ears, which lay back flat on his head every time it thundered.

"Don't you do something stupid, too," she said softly to her horse and patted his wet neck. She had to be careful that she didn't drop the slippery reins.

"I'll be so glad when we're home," Cathy said to Lillian, shivering with the cold.

"I'll be glad only when Josh and Kevin are home, too," replied Lillian and looked over at her girlfriend.

"Are you scared?" asked Cathy, and Lillian nodded.

"Hmm. You?"

"Very."

"Ricki probably feels the same. It's so horrible that this had to happen to Kevin. Sharazan is always so cool. Why did he have to spook during this night ride?"

"It's all because of this miserable thunderstorm!"

Cathy looked back over her shoulder and into the worried face of her girlfriend.

"Oh, man, Ricki looks terrible," she exclaimed. "How much longer will it take until we're back at the parking lot? I've completely lost my orientation."

Lillian shrugged her shoulders and lifted her eyes a little.

"I think at least another 15 minutes," she said. Then she stared straight ahead. She just didn't feel like talking anymore.

*

I can't stand it any longer, thought Ricki, and she clamped her fist tightly around the wet reins. *We're riding happily back home, and Kevin . . .* She began to cry softly, her tears mingling with the rain in her face.

Diablo raised his neck. He felt Ricki's restlessness and sensed that it wasn't because of the rain. Suddenly he stood still.

Ricki wanted to urge him forward when she realized that his stopping was a sign.

"Do you really think so?" she asked her horse softly. "Do you really think we should go back?"

Diablo remained motionless, and the riders in front of Ricki gradually got farther and farther ahead.

Once again, a brilliant flash of lightning crossed the sky and was immediately followed by a clap of thunder that almost broke Ricki's eardrums.

"Oh, Diablo, I'm scared…scared of this storm…scared about Kevin. God, tell me what I should do!"

Desperate and sobbing, Ricki wished hard that Kevin were at her side.

"Darn it, Kevin, where in the world are you?" Suddenly she saw him in her mind's eye. He lay somewhere in a meadow, not moving. Sharazan was nowhere to be seen.

"No!" Ricki shrieked.

"Where? Where are you?" she asked, but the image had already vanished.

She tried desperately to get the image back, tried to remember something about the area where she had seen Kevin in her mind, but it was in vain, and she found no answer to her question.

"I think I'm going crazy," said Ricki to herself.

Diablo turned his head around and looked at his rider from below.

What do you want? he seemed to be asking, and Ricki answered in her mind: *I want to find Kevin.*

Then what are you waiting for?

"Yeah, what *am* I waiting for?" Ricki said out loud, and then she turned Diablo around. "Let's go, my boy," she said. She avoided looking up at the sky for good reason: It was the worst thunderstorm she'd ever experienced.

Scared to death, she tried to ignore the flashes of lightning and claps of thunder and concentrate only on finding Kevin. Nevertheless, she jumped each time there was a crash from the heavens.

She kept thinking about her mother, who had explained to her, even as a small child, how to behave in a thunderstorm.

"Never go outside. Look for protection in a house, but never under a tree, much less in the woods. If you happen to be caught outside, crouch down or sit down. Put your head down and wrap your arms around your legs…make yourself as small as possible so that you aren't a target for the lightning. Don't run around, and never ride—do you hear me—never ride when there is a thunderstorm."

Ricki gulped for air. She felt that she was sinking into an ever-worsening panic.

"Diablo, tell me that nothing will happen to us. We're not out riding for fun in this weather. We have to find Kevin."

The girl swallowed hard and then bravely urged her horse forward. She tried to figure out in which direction Sharazan had run when he bolted from the barbecue area.

If he had galloped straight ahead, he would have ended up somewhere in the fields between the old brewery and the old country road, which had been closed for about two years. But where? Then again, maybe Sharazan had run in a curve.

Ricki's brain raced.

She estimated that she could save some time by taking a shortcut across the meadows instead of riding the whole way back to the barbecue pit. Of course, this could be dangerous. The ground would be soft, spongy, and uneven. She would be risking Diablo stepping into a concealed hole. But she didn't really have a choice. She had a feeling that Kevin needed help as quickly as possible.

Determined, she turned off of the trail with Diablo, and was glad that she had remembered to pack the little flashlight into her belt bag when she'd left home that day.

Mom was right, as usual, when she told me to take that stuff with me, thought Ricki as she let Diablo walk forward very slowly.

She leaned forward as far as she could and let the small circle of light from the flashlight shine directly in front of Diablo's hooves. She hoped that the horse would be better able to find his way.

For a moment she wondered whether she should dismount and lead Diablo, but she was terrified that the horse could get away from her and disappear into the darkness as well. Frightened, Ricki shook her head. No! She wasn't going to risk that.

Diablo seemed to have gotten used to the storm, or else

he just knew how important it was for Ricki that they keep moving. In any event, he was much calmer now. The confidence he now radiated seemed the opposite of what Ricki conveyed.

"Dear God, please let me find Kevin," prayed Ricki silently to herself while she rode on in the direction she hoped to find her boyfriend. It was much later—when she rode past a small chapel that was miles away from the old brewery, or so it seemed to her—that she realized she had lost her orientation in the darkness and had led Diablo onto a completely different trail.

That doesn't belong here, thought Ricki, looking at the small building, and she felt a pain in her heart. *That just can't be true! Oh, God, where on earth am I?*

Completely bewildered, she brought Diablo to a halt.

I'm totally lost, she screamed inside herself. *How is this possible? I rode straight ahead the whole time.*

Then Ricki suddenly remembered that there was a small wood behind the chapel. She would have to ride through it if she wanted to get to the old road that was closed.

Never look for protection under a tree, much less in a woods, and never ride—do you hear me—never ride when there's a thunderstorm.

In Ricki's head, thoughts were whirling about as though a thousand bumblebees had built a nest inside.

Mom, I have to go through there. I know I shouldn't do it, but it's for...for Kevin! God, please don't let anything bad happen. Please, please, she thought, and then, frightened to death, she steered her horse into the woods.

*

It seemed to her that hours had gone by since she had separated from the others, but it hadn't been more than 45 minutes since she had ridden away.

Untiringly, Diablo walked forward, although he could hardly see the trail under his hooves. He sensed how important it was for Ricki that he carry her as far as she wanted to go, and he felt the deep trust she had placed in him.

"We have to find him, my boy. Do you understand? We just have to. I'm so glad that you're here with me." Ricky bent down over his neck and buried her face in his wet mane, and then she pulled herself together and sat upright in the saddle.

Diablo had stopped for a moment when he no longer felt Ricki's weight on his back. Confused, he looked behind him.

What's wrong? he seemed to ask. Ricki patted his neck to comfort herself more than him.

"Everything's okay. Come, let's keep going."

Ricki's teeth were chattering. She had been soaked for quite a while and now she began to shiver. Her hands were wet and they were cramping around the reins. Her feet felt numb, her thighs felt icy, and her head felt as if it would burst with worry and fear for Kevin.

Ricki sniffed and wiped her eyes. *If only I weren't so tired,* she thought, and longed for her warm bed. But she was determined to continue searching until she found Kevin.

"Come, we have to go on," she whispered to her horse, and immediately he began to move. *You are amazing,* she thought, and kept trying to shine the flashlight on the ground in front of Diablo. If only they could find their way out of the woods.

Chapter 5

"Well, we made it," announced Ziggy, relieved, when he arrived at the parking lot at Echo Lake with the group of riders.

"Finally! I thought we'd never get here!" Cathy exclaimed, glad that the first part of their trek was over.

"Phew!" Lillian exhaled loudly, exhaustion mixed with relief. "Now all we have to do is get back ho—"

"We have enough horse transports here," called out Ziggy. "Those of you who rode here can put your horses in the trailers with the others. We'll drive you back home, naturally. I'm glad no one is out in this storm."

"Ziggy, that's so nice of you!" Cathy smiled with gratitude and turned around. "Ricki, did you hear that? We can...Ricki?"

"Ricki's missing!" she yelled suddenly, and Ziggy felt the ground fall away from under his feet.

"Say that again!"

"Ricki's missing! I have no idea how long! She was behind us 15 minutes ago!" Cathy's voice began to shake hysterically.

Lillian turned white as a ghost.

"Ricki's mother will kill us," she whispered and swallowed hard. "She will absolutely kill us. That I promise you!"

"Man, is she crazy?" Ziggy lost his cool entirely. "I'm sure she rode back to search for Kevin. What a stupid, insane thing to do, putting herself at risk like that. What do I do now? It's not enough that Kevin is missing. No, now that girl is also missing and in danger, too. This is going to drive me nuts!"

"Didn't I tell you that the kid—"

"Albert, for once in your life, shut up! All you ever do is complain!"

Ziggy made himself calm down, while he thought everything over feverishly.

"Well, first let's get the horses in the trailers and drive them and the younger riders home like we planned. Then I'll drive back and pick up Robby and Josh, and—please God—Kevin. Then we'll have to start looking for Ricki."

"How do you intend to get three or four horses in one transporter?" asked Albert, grinning nastily at Ziggy. The man really seemed to enjoy watching other people suffer and worry.

"We won't have to!" Lisa answered suddenly in an uncharacteristically harsh voice.

"Huh? What are you say—!"

"I'm going to follow behind Ziggy with our trailer, so that we can get all of the horses in! And don't you dare contradict me, Albert Perkins. Your behavior tonight has been absolutely intolerable!"

"Lisa, don't get excited!" Ziggy tried to calm down Albert's wife.

"I don't want to calm down!" said Lisa, furious. "Don't worry. I'll drive this old 'beer barrel' home, and put the

69

horses in the stable. Then I'll be right back to help with the others. Okay?"

Ziggy nodded thankfully.

"Good, let's meet here again, as quickly as possible…or maybe we should just drive toward the barbecue pit. We'll be sure to meet up along the way. Okay?"

Lisa nodded and pushed Albert into the car after the horses had been loaded into the trailer.

Gradually, the trailers left the parking lot, taking the kids home and the animals back to their dry stalls. The storm continued unabated.

Cathy and Lillian sat in the back seat of Nancy Bertram's car and held hands silently. Both of them were thinking the same thing.

How are we going to tell Ricki's mother that her daughter has disappeared and is outside in this terrible thunderstorm looking for Kevin?

Their only hope was that Nancy would be with them when they had to explain.

*

Susanna and Link had driven all around the area and had checked out all the roads and trails around the barbecue pit, but they had seen no sign of Kevin and Sharazan.

"This is crazy," repeated Link once again. "Sharazan would hardly have stayed on the trail. He would have galloped off into the distance—somewhere we can't follow with the car!"

"Could *you* just drive home calmly and go to bed if you knew that the boy is still out here somewhere?" Susanna asked.

"No, of course not. Keep driving. Let's start back at the beginning. Barbecue pit…turn right, turn left."

Susanna let the car roll to a stop and turned off the motor for a moment. Exhausted, she put her head down on her hands while keeping her grip on the steering wheel.

"Do you think he's hurt?" she asked quietly, and Link stroked her hair gently.

"I have no idea, Susanna, but I can see that you're hardly able to keep your eyes open. Come on, let's change places. I'll drive for a while, okay?"

Susanna nodded gratefully. Driving in this rain had really tired her eyes, and at the moment she felt she wouldn't be able to recognize Sharazan even if he was standing right in front of the car.

Awkwardly the young woman climbed over into the passenger seat, while Link raced around the car and, five seconds later, plumped down into the driver's seat soaking wet.

"The shower woke me up," he said, but he couldn't seem to make Susanna smile.

"Drive," she ordered him in a tired voice. "If something has happened to Kevin, we've got to find him. Do you hear me? We just have to!"

Link nodded silently and turned on the motor of the old camper.

"Here we go again," he said quietly, and the camper started to move slowly forward.

*

Sharazan had galloped blindly through the darkness. Suddenly he realized that the weight on one side had slid down slightly and was now starting to impede his legs.

The feeling reminded him of the time he was a circus horse and the "Hungarian Riders" had performed their tricks on his back. With the help of a few leather loops on the saddle, these riders had managed to climb down on one side and climb under his belly and up onto the saddle on the other side, while he was in full gallop. Sharazan noticed that his rider wasn't trying to get back into the saddle. The animal knew that something was wrong, but the heavy rain and the continuing thunderstorm had driven him farther and farther onward in an attempt to escape both.

Trembling from the exertion as well as fear, Sharazan suddenly stopped. His instincts told him he would not be able to get over the high, wide bushes in front of him, barely recognizable in the darkness, with this rider hanging on his back.

Breathing heavily, his nostrils puffed out, and with dangerous heaving, he turned his head back to his rider, who, with the last ounce of strength left in him, managed to free his foot from the stirrup and let himself fall down onto the soft, muddy ground, where he remained motionless.

Kevin hardly heard the next clap of thunder, which sounded muffled, as though his ears were stuffed with cotton. *I'm still alive,* was his last thought before he lost consciousness.

However, the thunder spooked Sharazan yet again, and he turned on his hind legs and took off into the darkness. By now, the full moon was completely covered with clouds, and all was black.

*

Something hurried by.

Diablo halted suddenly and raised his head.

Ricki had been much too concerned about Kevin to notice the small shadow. She became even more frightened as suddenly a huge flash of lightning illuminated the forest like daylight and she saw a fox cowering along the side of the trail.

Ricki shone the flashlight at the animal, and immediately it started to growl menacingly. But when at the next clap of thunder, it ran away into the woods, Ricki felt a great relief.

For a few seconds she wondered whether she should ride back or not, but clearly she was already in the middle of the woods, and the path that lay before her and would bring her to the road was the same distance as the path she had already taken.

"Forward, Diablo," she decided, despite the fact that she was shivering so much from cold and fatigue that she could hardly stay in the saddle. "God, I am so afraid. Kevin…Kev-viiin!" Her strength gone, she sank down over the neck of her horse and sobbed into his mane as the animal started to move again.

After a few yards, Ricki pulled herself together, sat upright, and tried to light the path for Diablo with her flashlight, although her hands were so cold she wasn't sure she could keep her grip on it.

When they came to bends or forks in the path, she had to make a split-second decision about which direction she should take. In her mind, she went through the rides she had made here in the past, trying to recall the trails, but in the darkness nothing looked familiar.

However, her courage returned when she realized that she'd been on the trail for a long time, and was pretty sure she'd reach the road in a few minutes. Through flashes of lightning she could see that the woods were becoming less dense. Suddenly she saw headlights in the distance, and her heart gave a little jump.

"Diablo, my boy, we made it! We're finally out of the woods," she said with a tired and shaky voice. But when she looked about her, she gasped. "Oh, no!" Completely confused, she pulled the reins tight and stared straight ahead.

"The chapel. Diablo, that's the chapel up ahead. We've been riding in a circle!"

Totally exhausted and downhearted, she sobbed quietly.

It's over, she thought despairingly. *Over, over, over! No chance now to find Kevin. Kevin, where in the world are you?*

"I want to go home. Please, please, Diablo, take me home." With these words, she let go of the reins. Letting them hang, she bent over and wrapped her arms around the horse's neck.

"I…can't…go…on," the words came out almost instinctively. "I…I…Diablo…" She just couldn't do any more. Her thoughts were a jumble and a horrible headache threatened to make her head explode.

Ricki began to drift. She was convinced that this was all just a bad dream and prayed that she soon would wake up from this nightmare. But as much as she tried to believe it was only a dream, the reality wouldn't go away.

Diablo sensed that his rider was no longer able to help him, so he began to trot more slowly and cautiously but with the confidence of one knowing exactly where he was going.

Ricki no longer cared which direction they went.

The storm hadn't let up, and she was wet, frozen, tired to the point of collapse, and her nerves were at the breaking point.

How could I have been so stupid to think that I would find Kevin? she asked herself, and then, a second later, she began to wonder where Sharazan had gone. But she was no longer able to concentrate. She just wanted to close her eyes and escape the whole situation.

Diablo kept going, and Ricki no longer paid any attention to which trail he took. In her mind's eye she saw the most horrible pictures, pictures of Kevin lying somewhere, too far away to be found by anyone.

Suddenly, her horse stopped trotting.

"What now?" she wondered.

Ricki sighed and then let the light from her flashlight play across the ground. She saw that Diablo had left the trail and his hooves were now sunk deep into the mud.

With her heart beating wildly, the girl dismounted. As tired as she was, she had to help her horse out of the mud.

"If only I knew how we were going to get out of here," Ricki said aloud, and called herself an idiot. She hadn't paid any attention to the path, and now she had another problem to deal with.

"I have no idea where we are. I can't see anything, and, oh, darn, what am I going to do?!"

Ricki pulled Diablo by the reins in order to get him to move forward, but the black horse just stretched out his neck. He didn't budge an inch in the desired direction.

"Diablo, please, come on. We can't stay here," begged Ricki, but Diablo remained stubborn. Then he turned his head away and pulled Ricki with him.

"Hey, what are you doing? Why are you turning around? Do you want to go back? Come on, that's not the right direction. Stand still."

Diablo had managed to turn himself completely around

75

and started back to the trail. The only thing Ricki could do was to follow him, stumbling and tired. It was hard not to lose her boots in the deep mud.

Groaning, crying, begging, and pleading she tried to get her horse to halt, but the horse refused to obey.

Why did I dismount? she asked herself. *Why was I such an idiot? If Diablo gets away from me, that will be the end.*

On the trail again, the horse was covering more and more ground. It almost seemed as though he had set himself a goal and no matter what, he was determined to reach it.

"God, I want to go home. Diablo! DIABLO! Where are you going?" Ricki was beginning to sound hysterical. Noticing the change in her voice, her horse put his ears back and whinnied.

The girl was trembling all over and could hardly put one foot in front of the other, but the fear that Diablo could get away gave her strength she didn't know she had, and allowed her to keep up with her horse. The last thing she wanted was for her beloved horse to break away and disappear into the night.

When Diablo shook his head violently, Ricki slipped on the muddy ground and lost her footing, causing her to drop her flashlight.

The horse urged her to go forward, much too fast, it seemed to her, so that she had no chance of retrieving her only source of light, which had gone out when she dropped the flashlight.

That's just great! Fabulous! Ricki thought desperately. *Things can't get much worse.*

While she tried to concentrate on how to get back in the saddle, the thunder and rain continued without interruption.

With one more brilliant flash of lightning and the following thunderclap, Diablo stopped and stood stone still, as though he were paralyzed. A loud whinny shook his body and scared Ricki almost out of her senses.

"No, Diablo! Don't!" she screamed in panic as the horse pulled her with him a few yards, constantly changing direction.

Then, suddenly, he stood still again and scratched the ground with his front hoof. He snorted excitedly and stretched out his neck, putting his head to the ground.

"What kind of game are you playing with me?" asked Ricki, about to collapse. She leaned into her horse. She took two or three deep breaths and decided to take advantage of the fact that Diablo was still to get back into the saddle, but then she thought she heard a small voice through the pounding rain.

She listened as hard as she could through the roar of the storm, but as much as she tried, there was nothing more to hear.

With a racing heart, she put her foot in the stirrup and started to pull herself up. But just then she heard some snatches of words in the wind.

"Help," said a voice from somewhere near. "Please…I'm over here."

"Kevin?!" Ricki stood next to her horse and tried to figure out where the voice was coming from. Was it possible that Diablo had brought her to her boyfriend? Was she really going to find him where no one had thought to look?

"Diablo, lead me there. You've brought me this far, please, find Kevin. Please." And as though the horse understood the pleas of his two-legged friend, he immediately started to move.

This time, Ricki didn't make any attempt to stop him. Trusting him completely, she stumbled beside him, although her feet were numb and her walking was unsure. She was convinced that Diablo was taking her directly to Kevin.

"Help!" she heard again, and goose bumps formed all over her.

"Kevin!" she screamed into the darkness. "KEVIN! Where are you? KEV–VIIIN!"

*

"We have to leave," said Josh, and patted Cherish on the neck to comfort her. "The weather is getting worse and worse. We can't wait here forever."

Robby nodded sadly.

"I think you're right. The chance that Kevin will ride back here is about one in a million. I don't like to think that he is somewhere out there in the dark, but we do have a responsibility to ourselves and our horses."

"Yeah, I get the feeling that Cherish isn't going to stay calm much longer. Let's go. I think the others are probably almost home by now, and I'm sure that one or the other of them will get a car and drive out here to look for Kevin. Maybe Susanna and Link will be lucky."

"Hmm, then they would have come back here and told us. Let's go. I'll be glad when the animals are back in their stalls."

Silently, the two young men tightened the saddle girths, mounted, and rode back along the designated trail. They weren't happy on horseback today either, and with each clap of thunder they shuddered.

"No more moonlight rides, said Josh, and Robby just ducked his head down between his shoulders, like a turtle.

"It was supposed to be an unforgettable ride," he replied softly. "We had imagined something really wonderful: the full moon, a summer night, the barbecue."

"Well, at least this ride will be unforgettable," Josh said sarcastically. "Although this ended somewhat differently from how it was planned."

Robby nodded dejectedly.

"I hope nothing has happened to Kevin. I would never forgive myself if it did."

Josh tried to keep up his friend's spirits.

"Oh, don't be ridiculous. We shouldn't even think of such a thing." He said lightly, but his thoughts were no less troubled than Robby's.

*

Josh and Robby had been on the trail for about 20 minutes when Ziggy came toward them with the horse trailer in tow.

"What's up?" he shouted as he jumped out of the car and opened the loading gate. "Did you hear or see anything of Kevin?"

Josh and Robby shook their heads no, and brought their horses to the trailer, where they loaded them as quickly as possible.

"What a mess!" barked Ziggy. "Ricki's gone, too! She probably took off to go look for her boyfriend!"

"What?" Josh turned pale and Robby felt his stomach lurch.

"That's just a bad joke, isn't it?"

"Do I look like I'm joking?" Ziggy's eyelids began to twitch from nervousness.

"That means that we have two riders to look for in this awful storm, doesn't it?"

"Looks like it. I thought Ricki was smarter than that. Is she crazy?" Josh was really upset, but Robby had quickly gotten himself under control again.

"What would you do if it were Lillian instead of Kevin?" he asked softly.

Josh said nothing. No question about it. Of course, he would look for her!

The three men got into the car, and Ziggy drove slowly back over the muddy path to the barbecue pit so that they could turn around.

When they were almost back to the parking lot at Echo Lake, they saw Lisa with her trailer driving toward them.

The young woman rolled down the window a bit so that she could talk to Ziggy. "I'm sorry it took so long. Albert ranted and raved for a while."

"The main thing is that you're here now," replied Ziggy. "I'm going to drive Robby and Josh and their horses home to the stalls, and then I'll come back as quickly as possible. Maybe you can look around here while I'm gone. It should be possible to find the horses at least. They're not so small that you can't see them, after all."

Lisa nodded and revved the engine a little too quickly, causing her tires to spin in the mud until they got traction; then the car moved forward with the trailer behind it.

"So, now let's get home as fast as possible," said Ziggy, more to himself than to his passengers, and he wiped the condensation from the inside of the windows with a cloth.

*

80

Brigitte Sulai sat at her kitchen table nervously twisting a handkerchief. Nancy Bertram put her hand on her shoulder comfortingly.

"Why?" asked Ricki's mother desperately. "Why does Ricki always have to take such risks, especially during such a terrible storm? She knows how dangerous that can be. She saw with her own eyes what can happen. My God, if she's struck by lightning, or if the horse bucks her off…or… Oh, I can't bear thinking about it," she sobbed.

Jake, who had been kept awake by the storm, too, sat at the table with his lips pressed together. He kneaded his scarred and callused hands restlessly, but avoided saying anything.

Don't get upset, he kept thinking. *The doctor said that you shouldn't get upset. I'm sure nothing terrible has happened. They'll all come back safe and sound. Just don't get excited.*

Instinctively he put his hand on his chest, over his heart, and felt a little pain.

Just not another heart attack, he kept thinking. *That would be the end. . .*

"I hope Marcus is lucky and finds the two of them," stammered Ricki's mother tonelessly. She got up and walked to the window, her knees shaking. She wished that her husband, who had left to look for Ricki and Kevin about two minutes ago, would appear laughing in the doorway with both of the missing kids beside him.

"I'm sure they'll be here any minute," Nancy said, trying once more to be reassuring. *Hopefully,* she added in her mind, before she left quietly.

*

81

In the meantime, Cathy and Lillian were rubbing Rashid and Doc Holliday dry in their stalls.

"We have to tell Kevin's mother," said Lillian suddenly, but Cathy replied, "That's impossible. You know she's spending the weekend at a spa with Carlotta, and cell phones aren't allowed."

"Didn't they leave a number where they can be reached in an emergency?"

"If they did, then Kevin has it."

After this short conversation, there was silence again. The two girls were busier with their horses than necessary, but they needed something to take their minds off their worries.

They had imagined this weekend was going to be perfect. They had planned to sleep in the Sulais' hayloft for the rest of the night after the ride, but now it would be impossible for them to close their eyes, even though they were completely exhausted.

After a while, there was simply nothing left to do, so the two girls wrapped themselves in horse blankets and sat down on bales of straw.

"We should change into something dry," said Lillian, shivering, but Cathy just looked at her with huge eyes.

"Our clothes are in Ricki's room. Do you feel like running into Ricki's mother right now?"

"Not really! I'd rather freeze," admitted Lillian and pulled the blanket even tighter around her body.

The two sat together in the stable for quite a while lost in thought and listening to the horses eating their extra ration of hay.

They didn't notice Brigitte enter the stable and stand in the doorway, her eyes red with tears, her skin as transparent as a ghost.

"Come inside," she said softly to Cathy and Lillian. "You should take a hot shower and change into dry clothes and then eat something. It won't help Ricki and Kevin if you two get sick."

The two girls got up hesitantly.

"Thanks, Mrs. Sulai," said Lillian. "I'm so sorry. I mean, the situation with Ricki—"

Cathy stuttered a few vague words, too, which got Brigitte to smile a little, if painfully.

"I knew something would happen during this ride," she said quietly. "Don't blame yourselves. It's not your fault. I shouldn't have allowed it. I—" Brigitte turned aside so that Ricki's friends wouldn't see her tears, but then she faced them and held her arms open to them.

"Come here, you two."

Lillian and Cathy looked uncertainly at each other before going to Brigitte, who wrapped her arms around them in a tight embrace.

"I'm very glad that at least you two are back safe and sound," she whispered as she and the girls left the stable.

If only Ricki and Kevin were back, too.

Chapter 6

"Hey! Stop! Did you see that? There's something over there." Susanna leaned so far forward in her seat that the tip of her nose almost touched the windshield of the camper.

"Where? I didn't see anything," Link answered. He put on the brakes immediately and the camper slowly rolled to a standstill.

They both stared sharply out of the windows, but the shadow Susanna had seen had already disappeared.

"What did you see?" Link asked.

"It looked like a horse," replied Susanna, as she opened the glove compartment to retrieve the flashlight.

"You're not going to get out in this storm just because you *might* have seen something, are you? Maybe it was just a deer."

"Deer!" Susanna tapped her finger on her forehead, then she turned up the collar of the old raincoat she'd pulled on and opened the door. "I hope that I can distinguish between a tiny deer and a gigantic horse," she said, and with that she hopped down from the high passenger seat into the mud.

"Wait here," she said quickly, before Link could raise any more objections. "I'll be right back."

"But—"

She shut the car door and hurried off in the direction where she'd seen the shadow disappear.

Link slammed his fist against the steering wheel.

"Women! They always have to do everything the hard way," he said out loud. Then he sighed, pulled the key out of the ignition, and left the camper, too.

"Wait, Susanna!" he called after her. "I'm coming with you." And he ran after her.

*

Marcus sat behind the wheel of his car with his lips pressed tightly together. For what seemed like hours now, he'd been driving around in the woods between the barbecue pit and Echo Lake, hoping to catch sight of his daughter.

He knew from Nancy that other riders were searching for the missing kids in their cars, but he soon realized that Ricki and Kevin could be anywhere. There were no clues as to their whereabouts. He also knew that Sharazan had bolted and galloped away, and Marcus understood his daughter well enough to know that she wouldn't come back until she had found Kevin.

On one hand, he was proud of his daughter. She'd gone after Kevin despite all the obvious dangers. But on the other hand he was upset that in her usual devil-may-care manner, she'd thrown caution to the wind and ridden off on an errand of mercy in this terrible storm.

"God, don't let anything happen to her—to either one of them," he prayed quietly, and continued to stare into the darkness as he drove slowly along. He knew he couldn't go home to Brigitte without Ricki. She would have a nervous breakdown, he was sure of that. Brigitte had never felt comfortable around horses and always worried that something would happen when Ricki went off riding. And a few times it did. Ricki had caused her family worry before.

For a moment, Marcus wondered whether it had been such a good idea to let his daughter have her own horse. Ever since Diablo had entered the lives of the Sulai family, something was always happening to Ricki. She seemed to stumble from one adventure to the next with that horse.

Marcus glanced at his watch. It was 1:27 a.m. Desperate, he groaned loudly.

Thirteen! he thought, his heart aching. *She's only 13! My God, I should have listened to Brigitte.*

*

Lisa continued driving straight ahead. It was hard to keep the car on the road. One of the windshield wipers had stopped working and now she had only a limited view out the window.

She didn't feel comfortable being out in this storm alone. So she was relieved to discover Susanna's camper, which Link has just left in the middle of the road. He hadn't bothered to park it at the side, believing it was extremely unlikely that anyone else would be driving along this road at this time of night.

Lisa honked the horn to signal to Link and Susanna that she had arrived. After a few seconds, she realized that the camper in front of her was empty.

"Where did they go?" Lisa mumbled to herself. There must have been a good reason to make the two of them get out of the camper in this awful weather. Maybe they had found Kevin.

86

The young woman decided to wait in her car. What else could she do? She had little choice. She didn't feel like being out in the darkness all alone, but she couldn't turn around or go back either.

*

Sharazan whinnied loudly as he heard crackling steps in the brush nearby.

"I was right! Link! There really is a horse!" Susanna punched her friend in the ribs.

"One to nothing for your good eyesight," admitted Link softly. "I just hope Sharazan doesn't bolt when we get near him."

Carefully the two made their way toward the animal. Strangely he didn't look as though he were going to bolt.

"Sharazan," called Susanna in a reassuring voice. "Sharazan, good boy. Don't move. We'll be right there. There's nothing to be afraid of, everything's okay. Do you hear us? Everything's okay."

Slowly, with her hands outstretched, Susanna kept walking. She could barely see the silhouette of Kevin's horse. He was standing as still as a statue.

The young woman kept talking to the animal until she was close enough to grab his bridle. Relieved, she patted the horse on his neck reassuringly.

"I've got him, Link. Darn it, his reins are all tangled up in the branches. Link?"

"I'm already here, lovely lady. Your knight in shining armor has arrived!"

"Idiot!" laughed Susanna, but she was glad that Link was with her and had already started to untangle the

87

reins so that she could concentrate solely on calming the horse.

"Done! We can go. Should I take him?" Link held out his hand, and Susanna was glad to turn over the huge animal to him. Link would be much better able to hold on to him when the bolts of lightning started to flash across the sky.

Together the three walked back to the camper.

"How are we going to get him home?" Susanna asked with a concerned look.

"A completely different question," countered Link, "is where did our boy here leave Kevin?"

*

Lisa had left her lights on and dozed off. All this excitement had left her in a state of anxiety. Scared to death, she jumped when someone knocked on her window.

"Hey, super, you're here!" Susanna resembled a forest gnome, with her long hair plastered against her face. And Link didn't look any better.

Relieved that she wasn't alone any longer, Lisa sprang out of the car and listened as the couple caught her up on the situation.

"And where is Kevin?" she asked as Link lead Sharazan to the trailer behind her car while she and Susanna opened the loading gate.

"We've no idea." Resignation showed on Susanna's face, and shivering with cold, she wrapped her arms around her body.

"You didn't happen to see Ricki and Diablo, did you?" asked Lisa.

"What?" Susanna thought she had heard wrong. "Don't tell me Diablo bolted as well?"

Lisa shook her head. "No, not that, but Ricki. Sometime during the ride back she got separated, probably went to find Kevin. We only noticed it when we had arrived at the parking lot."

"Oh, no!" Link clapped the loading ramp up. After giving this new wrinkle a few moments thought, he said, "Well, we must get Sharazan home first so that at least he's safe and dry."

"And then?"

"Well, *what* then?" Link didn't know what he should answer.

"To be honest, I almost fell asleep at the wheel a while back."

"Then drive home after leaving Sharazan. It's okay," said Susanna, and she nodded encouragingly at Lisa.

"Do you really think so? You know…Albert is so…"

"It's really okay!" Link nudged Lisa gently toward her car and held the door open. "Get going, and see that you get to bed! Thanks for everything."

Lisa managed a weary smile and got in the car. She was more than happy that she would soon be in her warm bed. How she would ever get to sleep was another thing. She couldn't stop thinking about Ricki, Kevin, and Diablo, who were all still missing.

*

Ricki struggled beside Diablo. Kevin's calls were getting clearer, and the girl was certain he wasn't too far from her.

"Kevin!" she shouted again and again, and was ecstatic

when she finally heard "Ricki . . . here!" over the wailing of the wind.

Suddenly, the thunderstorm, which up to now had her frightened out of her wits, was forgotten. What were lightning and thunder against the certainty that she had finally found her Kevin?!

Abruptly Diablo came to a halt, almost causing Ricki to lose her balance.

She listened again intensely.

"Where are you?"

"Here, right here."

Judging by the distance of his voice, Ricki guessed that Kevin was less than 30 yards in front of her. Holding on to Diablo's reins, she ran as fast as she could toward him.

"Kevin! Kevin! I'm so relieved I've found you!" Tears of joy ran down her cheeks as she sank to her knees beside her boyfriend. "Are you okay? Say something."

Trembling, she stroked his face, which she could hardly see in the darkness and rain.

Kevin took a breath and shuddered. He had to admit to himself that during the past few hours he had come face to face with feelings of fear and uncertainty.

"How did you get here?" he asked, his voice flat and scratchy from calling for help all this time.

"Diablo led me here! He must have somehow known where you were!" Ricki was still kneeling on the ground. "Why are you lying down? Are you injured?"

Kevin moved a little and then winced. "I…I don't really know. My head hurts so much, and when I try to get up, I feel really dizzy. I must have hit my head on something when I fell off of Sharazan. Where is he, anyway? I hope nothing has happened to him."

Ricki's hands felt around on the ground.

"There's a big rock lying near your head," she discovered.

"Where is Sharazan?" Kevin insisted, worry in his voice. Ricki understood how he felt. It hadn't been that long ago that she'd been searching for Diablo, who'd run off through the brush when he'd freed himself from his rope.

"He probably ran home," Ricki tried to reassure her friend, but she knew that Kevin wouldn't believe her.

"Come," she said, putting an arm around his waist. "You have to try to get up. How long have you been lying here?"

"No idea. Ow! My leg – I must have pulled a muscle." Kevin, who had carefully sat up, tried to put his weight on his foot, jerked, and fell back onto the muddy ground.

"I am so sick to my stomach," he groaned in a voice so dismal that it stabbed at Ricki's heart. Then he started coughing and couldn't stop.

"You have to stand up," she pleaded with him while the rain continued beating down on them. "We have to get home somehow."

"I can't!"

"You have to!"

"I…can't…do it!"

Ricki coaxed her boyfriend, trying to persuade him, but Kevin just waved her away. Suddenly she got up and angrily stamped the ground with her foot, making the mud fly.

"Why do you think I've been riding for hours in this awful weather, scared to death at each flash of lightning, instead of being home asleep in my warm bed? Do you think I've been riding around just for fun? Are you insane? You have to get up, do you understand me?"

Kevin, taken aback by her sharp reply, gave a little nod

and a weak, "Yeah," before he very slowly, and with Ricki's help, finally stood up.

"Everything is spinning around. I feel nauseated." He leaned on his girlfriend's shoulder and took a few limping, stumbling steps and then stopped.

"Please, Ricki, I have to sit down again or else I'll fall down!"

Ricki held on to him, her arm wrapped tightly around him, and she lead Diablo with her other hand.

"Wait a minute," she said. She had an idea. If Kevin could climb into Diablo's saddle, they would be able to move much more quickly than if he had to sit down after every three steps.

"You have to get up on Diablo. Otherwise, I don't think we'll be able to get home today." Determined, she pushed and pulled Kevin to Diablo's side.

"Come on, I'll help you. But you have to help me a little. You're too heavy for me to heave you up into the saddle."

Kevin moaned. His pain was worse than Ricki thought. Although he felt as though he was going to faint, he grit his teeth and, with tremendous effort, pulled himself up into Diablo's saddle. Immediately he fell forward onto the horse's neck and stayed there.

Ricki relaxed a little when her friend was finally atop the horse. Carefully, slowly, she urged Diablo onward in the direction she thought would get them back home.

Worried, she kept glancing at Kevin. He was so weak that he didn't respond to any of her questions. So she decided to let him rest there and concentrated all of her strength on getting him back home.

*

Robby and Josh had brought their horses back to their stalls. After the animals had been taken care of, the young men got into Robby's car and drove to the Sulais' stable. First of all, Josh wanted to make sure Lillian had arrived there okay, and secondly, they both hoped they would find Kevin, Ricki, and their horses safe and sound.

They arrived just as Lisa was leading Sharazan out of the trailer.

The stable was lit up, as were the house and the yard, which meant they were all up and expecting Lisa, who had called them from her cell phone.

Cathy and Lillian, who had run into the stable as soon as they heard Lisa's car, were standing next to Jake, who took Sharazan and led him to his stall.

Josh's face lit up when he saw the horse. Playfully, he punched his friend in the arm.

"Hey, it looks like they've found Kevin. Man, I'm so glad." Beaming with happiness, he jumped out of the car after Robby had come to a slow stop on the wet gravel. He ran toward the stable door and wrapped his arms around Lillian, who smiled wearily at him.

"Well, everything okay again?" he asked, then his eyes widened when he saw that Diablo's stall was empty.

"Oh, no! Don't tell me Ricki still isn't back!"

Lillian shook her head.

"No, she's still out there, and Kevin's still missing, too," Cathy said, sniffing back her tears. "Susanna and Link found Sharazan, but there's no trace of the other two. Ricki's dad already drove off to look for them. Oh, Josh, I'm so scared." Cathy began to sob and leaned against his shoulder.

Anxiety was showing on Lillian's face as well, so Josh put his arms around both girls and pulled them close.

"Don't worry, you two, they'll turn up," he said softly, but his voice lacked its usual confident tone.

"I'm glad that you're back and safe," Lillian whispered, and cuddled close to her boyfriend. She held on to his hand tightly, as though she would never let go again.

Lisa waved good-bye and didn't mind when there wasn't a response. She understood that her riding companions had other worries at the moment.

"We could drive off again and help search for them," Robby thought out loud, but Jake, who was rubbing Sharazan down with hay and a rag to dry him off, shook his head firmly.

"Absolutely not! First of all, you don't have any idea where to look, and secondly, it won't help anyone if you drive into a tree because you're overtired! No, either you stay here or drive straight home." The old man stopped working for a minute and looked at the two young men seriously. "It's almost impossible to find anyone in the dark," he added and waited for them to agree, but Robby and Josh looked at each other knowingly.

"Okay, then we'll go back home," Robby said slowly. "Actually, I'm dead tired. Josh, are you coming? I'll drop you off."

Josh nodded and removed himself from the two girls, who had calmed down a little.

"Don't worry," Josh whispered to his girlfriend conspiratorially. "We're going to keep on looking anyway, but don't say anything to Jake. Okay?"

Lillian looked up at him gratefully. She would have been surprised if Josh had given up so easily, and besides, she felt much better knowing that there were two more people out looking for Kevin and Ricki. She was sure her two friends were lost somewhere in the dark and had no idea how they were going to get back home.

*

The thunderstorm had abated somewhat, but it was still pouring, and the air was a few degrees colder.

Ricki shivered all over and had to force herself, one step at a time, to keep on walking.

She kept glancing at Kevin with increasing concern. His body had begun to radiate heat despite the chilly night air. Sweat mingled with rain on his forehead, and he had difficulty staying in the saddle.

We'll never make it home, thought Ricki in desperation, and patted Diablo's wet neck. She no longer had any sense of time, especially since she couldn't see her watch in the dark.

"Kevin? Kevin! Don't you dare fall asleep!" She pleaded with him urgently, and was relieved when she heard a mumble as an answer.

Diablo seemed not to tire. He followed Ricki willingly, wherever she led him, although he must have asked himself, *Why isn't she taking the direct path toward home?* His instincts told him they were going in the wrong direction.

"If it weren't for you—" the girl whispered, and leaned against the black horse to gather strength. "There's only one horse in the world like you." Gratefully she stroked her hand across his soft nose, which was blowing out warm breaths that were visible in the cool night air.

Ricki sighed deeply, releasing some of the built-up tension, before she forced herself to go on. Strangely, she kept thinking of the most banal things. *I forgot to clean my room yesterday. I wonder where Harry went with Chico? I wonder whether the swallows in the nest above the tack room have hatched yet?*

Ricki knew she wouldn't be able to go on much longer. Her eyes scanned the darkness closely, but as hard as she tried she couldn't recognize any landmarks.

Diablo, who had walked patiently beside her up 'til now, began to urge her to go in another direction.

"Don't start anything, my good boy. Don't forget that Kevin is sitting on your back!" Ricki said softly, but she knew that she was no longer strong enough to oppose the will of the horse, so she gave in and followed him.

He knows what he's doing, she thought. *He did lead me to Kevin.* So she let Diablo pull her along.

After a short time, the horse stopped.

"What's the matter now?" asked Ricki. "Do you want to stay here for the night?" She sounded a little angry, but then she saw that Diablo had lead her to a hay barn, which suddenly appeared out of nowhere, and stood before her like a giant shadow. In this weather and in her condition, it seemed like a palace to her.

"You're wonderful, Diablo!" she sobbed, giving her horse a kiss on the nose. She pulled him behind her, and felt with one hand along the barn wall to find the door. After a few minutes she found it, and, with a little effort, she got it open.

Carefully she entered with Diablo, Kevin lying limply over his neck, and hoped that there was no farm machinery stored inside to bar their way. It looked as though the barn was empty except for a few bales of straw and hay.

Ricki sighed with relief, glad to have found shelter.

Of course, she could see less than she could outside, but

that didn't matter. The important thing was that they had a roof over their heads that gave them protection against the pouring rain—except in the places where the roof leaked pretty badly.

Kevin groaned softly.

"Are we home?" he asked, completely exhausted. Ricki swallowed hard in sympathy with her friend.

"No, I have no idea where we are, but at least we can rest here, and it's dry," she said gently as she felt for his hands.

Heavens, they're really hot, she thought, frightened. *He has a fever.*

"Come, you have to get down first." Gingerly she shook his leg a little when Kevin didn't even respond.

"Did you hear me? You have to get down from Diablo. There are some bales of straw you can lie down on."

Kevin sat up a little, but it was impossible for him to lift one leg over the saddle. He simply didn't have enough strength left.

Ricki had tears in her eyes.

"Come, just slide down one side to me. I…I'll hold on to you really tight. "

"Much…too…heavy," breathed Kevin, but Ricki just took hold of him and very slowly pulled him down. With all the strength left in her, she actually managed to get him safely onto the ground, although at the end, she fell down with him.

Diablo stood like a statue until he felt that Kevin was no longer in the saddle. Only then did he take three steps to the side, unconsciously helping Ricki with her task.

"Stand still, good boy…really great," she tried to comfort her horse, but Diablo was the only one of the three who was absolutely calm.

Panting, Ricki knelt beside Kevin, who lay still as though unconscious.

Gradually Ricki's eyes became accustomed to the darkness around her, and she was able to make out the bales of hay.

After she had caught her breath, she shoved a few of the bales together in order to make a kind of mattress for Kevin.

With a lot of effort, she pulled her boyfriend onto the temporary bed so that he didn't have to lie on the cold, damp ground.

Drained by her exertions, everything Ricki did, she did very slowly. Her limbs were stiff and hurt every time she moved, and she, too, felt that she was about to fall down exhausted. In addition, she began to feel really hungry, although she was amazed that she could feel anything like that after the ordeal she had gone through.

Diablo snorted, and Ricki heard him tremble.

"Wait," she said, unbelievably tired. "Where are you? Ah, good boy. Don't move. I'll take your saddle off. Stand still…that's better. Stop the snaffle, too. You've had this thing on long enough. I hope the wet leather hasn't rubbed too hard."

Ricki needed more time than usual for this maneuver because her numb fingers kept sliding off the wet leather straps, but nevertheless, she managed to accomplish this, too.

The girl felt as if her arms would touch the ground as she struggled to carry the saddle over to the straw bales.

Carefully she lifted Kevin's head and shoulders and shoved the saddle underneath to act as a pillow.

"Is that okay? Is that better or would you rather lie flat?" she asked quietly, but Kevin gave her no definite answer.

His chest rose and fell, rattling and whistling in quick breaths, making Ricki really frightened.

"What should I do? What should I do?" she agonized, while she held Kevin's limp, feverish hand and stroked it gently.

The boy's whole body was trembling, and he continued to sweat profusely.

"Chills and fever!" mumbled Ricki to herself, and it reminded her of the last episode she had seen of the medical series she watched on TV every Friday, the one where one of the actors was sick with pneumonia.

"And what to do now?" she kept asking herself, and then she tugged three more bales over to Kevin's temporary bed to make it wider.

Carefully, she lay down beside her boyfriend and put her arm around him to warm him and comfort him.

"Everything's going to be okay, Kevin. Stay calm. I'm here." Silently the girl wept.

"We should never have taken part in this ride," she whispered in the darkness. Suddenly she felt Diablo's warm breath in her hair.

"I'm so glad you're here with me." Lovingly she stroked his nose, and then the animal took a few steps away and began to eat the hay scattered on the barn floor.

Chapter 7

Marcus stopped his car at the Echo Lake parking area because he didn't know where else to look.

One after the other, Ziggy, Josh and Robby, and Susanna and Link arrived. They had used this area as the meeting place to start out on the late-night ride, so it was possible that Ricki or Kevin would turn up here sometime.

Marcus was grateful to the young people for their determined help in the search, even though he had blamed Ziggy and Robby at first.

"So, you two had the bright idea to organize this crazy ride? Terrific! Have you ever heard of supervision and responsibility? Did you know that those in charge had the responsibility to see that the minors got home safe and sound? You don't seem to take your responsibilities too seriously!"

Ziggy and Robby looked at each other with guilt. They knew better than to say anything. Marcus was about ready to explode.

But he pulled himself together quickly when he realized that the most important thing was to get organized and develop a plan that would help them find the kids.

"We've been driving back and forth here for three hours. We've searched this area as thoroughly as we could from our cars," reported Link, leaving out the fact that they had almost lost the exhaust pipe when they'd driven down a bumpy, rutted trail.

Marcus looked in Susanna's pale, worn face.

"You're completely exhausted, young lady," he said softly. "The rest of you, too. Go, drive on home now. I'm going to keep looking, although I probably won't be any luckier than you were. It'll be light in a few hours, and we'll have a better chance of finding them then."

Josh looked at the others and then took a step forward.

"Mr. Sulai, we *are* dead tired, but Ricki and Kevin...well, we won't be able to sleep until they're found," he said, and his riding companions nodded in agreement.

"But, you . . . " Marcus began again.

Ziggy didn't let him continue. He shook his head decisively.

"No buts. I wouldn't have a single moment of peace. We're going to keep searching!"

Ricki's father nodded gratefully.

"Then, let's not lose any time. We'll meet back here in...let's say, an hour? If anyone finds the kids, honk your horn to let the rest of us know, okay?"

"Good!"

"All set!"

"Thank you all for your help. I—" Marcus swallowed hard, overcome by his emotions.

"Let's go! We can talk later!"

Josh and Link gave each other a high-five as they passed on the way to their cars.

"So long."

"Here we go!"

Marcus waited until the young people were back in their cars and then waved at them before they drove off once again. All of a sudden, he regretted having yelled at Robby and Ziggy. After all, he could have prevented Ricki from going along.

Clara, Marcus thought suddenly. *If Clara were still alive, we'd know where the two of them are.*

Ricki's father sighed, then turned on the motor and opened his window slightly so that he could hear a car horn should one of the others find them.

Before he drove off, he pulled out his cell phone and dialed his home number. He hoped there might be some news there, but he could tell by Brigitte's voice, when she answered, that there was nothing new to report.

After a few comforting words, he said good-bye and put the phone on the seat beside him. Once again, he traced back over the riding trail, which he now knew by heart.

Another hour went by, during which he kept praying that his daughter would be found safe. The hour hand of his watch gradually approached 3 a.m. Marcus thought about Brigitte, who was at home, standing by the window waiting for them to return. He was sure that she was worried sick about Ricki, too, and wished he could take her in his arms and comfort her.

*

Lillian and Cathy sat on Ricki's bed wrapped in blankets. Brigitte had gently urged the two girls into her daughter's room to rest. They could hardly keep their eyes open any longer.

"There's no sense in you two becoming so tired that you can't stand up anymore. That won't make Ricki come home any faster," she said with tears in her eyes. She gave the girls extra blankets for warmth.

After Brigitte left the room, however, the two girls just sat on the bed like zombies, unable to get Ricki out of their thoughts.

They had been sitting there for almost an hour and had imagined the most awful, gruesome things that could have happened to Ricki and Kevin.

After a long period of silence, Cathy asked in a shaky voice, "You know what?"

"No, how could I?" responded Lillian wearily.

"I was so tired the whole time. All I wanted was to get into my warm bed, but now…now I'm wide awake, or at least in some kind of weird never-neverland I can't even describe." Cathy fell back on the bed and folded her arms behind her head.

"I feel the same way. I think I'm just too tired to sleep, and anyway, I think I would have a bad conscience if I just fell asleep while Ricki is out there somewhere in this awful weather." Lillian leaned back a little, too.

"At least the thunderstorm has let up and it's just raining now," said Cathy, and looked out the window. "I just can't understand how Ricki could take off on her own. She's so afraid of lightning and thunder."

"I think if someone you love is in trouble, you can even overcome your fears," explained Lillian, who was thinking about her Josh, for whom she, too, would go anywhere if need be.

"But she could have said something to us," Cathy began again. "After all, the two of us would have said something."

Lillian looked her girlfriend in the eyes.

"Do you really believe that?" she asked.

"Why not?"

"Well, I suppose we would have tried to stop her from doing it, and she knew that. That's why she did it without telling us!"

Cathy, weak with fatigue, slowly sat up, eased herself off the bed, and walked over to the window. Looking absentmindedly off into the distance, she said softly, "I wish I could go out and look for her, too."

"So do I," answered Lillian and stood behind her friend. "But can you imagine what would happen if we went missing, too?" Instinctively she embraced her younger friend and held her tight, both taking comfort in the closeness.

"They'll come back safe and sound, won't they?" Cathy asked so softly that Lillian could hardly hear her.

Lillian closed her eyes for a moment and sighed. She was as worried as Cathy.

"I'm sure they'll come home! Now let's try to get a little sleep; the night will be over sooner than we think."

Cathy nodded and let Lillian lead her back to the bed.

They lay down side by side, Lillian keeping her arm protectively around Cathy.

"Thanks," murmured Cathy after the older girl had turned out the light. "You're a wonderful friend. I'm glad I'm not alone!"

Lillian swallowed hard and kissed her on the forehead. So was she.

While Cathy gradually drifted off to sleep, Lillian lay awake for a long time staring into space. She listened intently in the darkness, hoping that she would hear a car, but other than the rain beating on the windows, there was nothing to hear.

*

Ricki, who was determined to stay awake at Kevin's side, was overcome by her extreme weariness nonetheless, and had fallen into a restless sleep. Strange, horrifying dreams went through her mind.

She was freezing and shivering, trying to keep warm, but in that cold barn, in wet clothing, it wasn't possible to maintain a normal body temperature.

Still asleep, Ricki moved close to Kevin and felt the trembling of his body. He had been lying on the cold, wet ground too long and his body was now showing the strain.

Ricki was dimly aware that it had begun to thunder again in the distance, but was too exhausted to pay attention to the warning sign of yet another thunderstorm.

Only when Diablo showed his unrest by whinnying shrilly and stamping on the ground did she sit up. Her heart beating wildly, she looked around her, confused at first, and then she realized what had happened and where they were.

"Oh, no! Not again!" Ricki sat on the bale of straw as though she were rooted to it. She was too afraid to move.

The storm had renewed itself, becoming even more powerful than before. The wind blew through the barn, coming through the cracks and holes between the clapboards as though they were made of paper. And the rain came through the many holes in the roof like a giant showerhead, something Ricki hadn't noticed when they arrived because the rain wasn't as heavy then.

A chill ran down her spine as a great bolt of lightning

flashed across the sky and lit up the inside of the barn. The lightning was immediately followed by a tremendous clap of thunder.

Ricki couldn't remember ever having gone through such a terrible night before, where one strong thunderstorm was followed by an even stronger one and the rain never stopped, as though it meant to flood the whole world.

Diablo paced back and forth inside the barn, and Ricki hoped the owner hadn't left a pitchfork lying around that could injure her horse if he stepped on it.

"Calm down, my darling, we're safe. Nothing can happen to us," she tried to comfort her horse, although she wasn't convinced herself.

Worried and afraid, she felt her way to Kevin, who had awakened at the crack of the thunder.

"What's happening?" he asked quietly and pressed Ricki's hand.

"You're awake? Do you feel any better?"

"I'm not sure. I feel as though my head is going to burst. It's so hot in here."

Ricki stroked a strand of hair back off his forehead.

"I think you have a fever," she told him, and then turned her attention to Diablo, who was still pacing around restlessly.

Suddenly Ricki got up.

"Don't ask me why, but I'm going to saddle Diablo. This storm and what's happening in the sky are starting to scare me."

"Diablo? Why is Diablo here?" Kevin asked, surprised. With great effort he tried to get up.

"He brought you here," explained Ricki. "Don't tell me you don't remember that?"

Kevin didn't say anything. He had a complete lapse of memory regarding the past hours. The last thing he remembered was the moment when Ricki had found him.

"Diablo, where are you? Come here, my good boy. Yeah, that's my good boy." Ricki held her horse by his mane and led him to the straw bed, where she slowly and carefully slid the saddle out from under Kevin's head. She put in the snaffle so that she could hold on to the horse and then she put the saddle on his back. The saddle blanket was still pretty wet, sending a cold shiver down the horse's spine.

"I'm sorry, Diablo, but at the moment there's nothing I can do about it." She tightened the saddle girth carefully, and then, still holding onto the reins, she sat down next to Kevin.

"Why did you saddle up?" asked Kevin as he examined his surroundings as though through a dense fog.

Ricki just shrugged her shoulders.

"I've no idea, it's just, well—"

At that moment, there was a clap of thunder right overhead. It was so ferocious that it felt as if the barn was being shaken apart.

"Oh, man!" she yelled. "I just knew it, somehow! GET OUT! Kevin! C'mon! We've got to get out of here! RIGHT NOW!"

Kevin stared at his girlfriend, but he couldn't seem to understand what she was telling him.

"What?"

"GET OUT! Kevin!" yelled Ricki again, and she grasped the boy by the hand and pulled him awkwardly to his feet.

"I'm so dizzy…slow…I…"

"C'mon! Get up on Diablo! Hurry up!" Without listen-

107

ing to Kevin's objections, she pushed him toward the horse, bent down, lifted the boy's foot, and put it into the stirrup.

Kevin stumbled a little, but Ricki used all of her strength and gave him a shove so that he landed up on the saddle faster than he wanted to.

"Hold on!" Ricki ordered. She heard the beams of the barn start to creak ominously. Without thinking about it, she pulled Diablo in the direction she thought the door was and felt around with her hand along the boards.

There! Finally! She found the bolt and pushed the door open against the wind. She pulled Diablo outside, with Kevin sitting on top very wobbly.

Less than two minutes later, the roof of the old barn gave way and collapsed.

Ricki's heart raced when she saw the ruins of the former hay barn in the light of the next bolt of lightning. The last lightning bolt had struck the tall tree next to the barn, splitting open the trunk and causing part of the treetop to fall on the roof. She remembered her childhood trauma and began to tremble.

"That was close," she whispered softly. "Everything okay?"

Kevin just nodded, but, of course, Ricki couldn't see that in the darkness.

"Okay," she said, strength and determination creeping back into her voice, "we can't avoid it any longer. We've got to get home, and we've got to get there in a hurry."

She began to lead her horse, but he tossed his head and turned in a completely different direction.

I thought you wanted to go home, he seemed to say, and then started to move forward.

"All right," Ricki agreed begrudgingly. "I think you'll find the way on your own much better than I could. Well, let's go."

With her knees still weak from the shock she had just experienced, she jogged beside her horse, who was trotting onward without hesitation. Ricki could hardly keep up.

Within a very short time, all three were soaking wet, and Ricki jumped with every clap of thunder.

Is it ever going to end? she asked herself. Her deepest wish was to get her injured friend home as quickly as possible and then fall into bed herself. She knew that her nerves would not be able to stand this stress much longer. It had been going on for hours now, and her growing fear of this new thunderstorm was making it worse.

*

"Who *knows* where they are!" Ziggy shrugged his shoulders with resignation and then looked at the others, shaking his head.

"In this pitch blackness, we can't see any farther than the beams of the headlights," added Josh.

Depressed, Ricki's father nodded.

Another hour of unsuccessful searching had gone by and, back at the parking lot, it was obvious the young people were visibly tired. Susanna could hardly keep her eyes open. Nevertheless, she said, "We were lucky that we found Sharazan, but, they have to be somewhere. They can't just have disappeared off the face of the earth. We have to keep looking."

Marcus inhaled deeply and bit his lip. Of course Susanna was right, but there was no sense in just going back and forth along the same roads, without being able to see in the distance in all directions.

"Please, I want you all to drive home now. At the moment, there's no use continuing." Ricki's father shined the flashlight on his watch. "It's after 4 a.m. It'll be light in about an hour and a half, and then it'll be easier."

"Okay, we'll continue the search at 5:30 a.m.," decided Robby, and his companions nodded in agreement.

"You all should get some sleep," Marcus said, looking at Susanna with concern.

"We can sleep after Ricki and Kevin have been found! If I go to bed now, I won't be able to do anything for the rest of the day. It's better if I just stay up, but I really need a cup of coffee—hot, black, and strong! Then I'll be just fine again!" grinned Susanna. Link just rolled his eyes.

"Exactly! Coffee! We could go to—"

"All of you, get in your cars, we'll drive to my house! Brigitte makes great coffee!" Marcus winked at the others. A cup of coffee at this time of night was the least he could do for the riders after all their help.

"Wonderful, Mr. Sulai, that's a terrific idea!" Robby shook Ricki's father's hand gratefully.

"I should have thought of it sooner," grumbled Marcus softly, and then everyone got into their cars and followed him. This seemed like the longest night of his life.

*

Lillian sat up suddenly. She thought she heard a noise outside. Wasn't there something?

"Hey, Cathy, wake up!" Vigorously, she shook her girlfriend by the shoulder.

"What's up? Did something happen?" Cathy jumped up, frightened.

"Listen! Don't you hear that? It sounds like a whole convoy of cars driving up to the house!"

Both girls hurried to the window.

"It's true! C'mon, let's go downstairs!" Lillian ran past Cathy, flung the door open, and ran down the steps. She stopped at the bottom landing.

Brigitte was standing in the doorway with her hands folded across her chest. Eyes full of fear, she looked toward the cars, and Marcus hated to have to tell her that Ricki and Kevin still hadn't been found.

Slowly he got out of the car, glanced at Brigitte, and then lowered his gaze and shook his head sadly.

Ricki's mother swallowed hard, then covered her face with her hands and turned and walked back into the house.

"Well? What's happened? Are they finally here?" Cathy ended up behind Lillian at the bottom of the stairs. Lillian gestured to her to be quiet.

The older girl went to Brigitte and wrapped her arms around her.

"Mrs. Sulai, I'm sure—sure—that she has found someplace where she's sheltered from the rain and where she isn't visible from the roads. I'm sure…"

"It's okay, Lillian." Ricki's mother fought against her tears and then all at once she burst out, "She's so frightened of thunderstorms, and now, now she's all alone out there."

"But she has Diablo," Cathy dared to respond, looking helplessly at Lillian.

"DIABLO!" Brigitte's head spun around. "That horse is to blame for everything! If it weren't for that horse, Ricki would be home safe in her bed and wouldn't have to deal

111

with all these dangers and fears! I hate that horse. If anything happens to my little girl…!"

Marcus arrived just in time to take Brigitte to their room before she could throw the china horse statue Ricki loved so much against the wall in a rage.

The riding companions looked awkwardly at each other, embarrassed. Cathy and Lillian had never seen Ricki's mother like this. Up until now she had been able to hide her fears whenever Ricki went riding, but today was obviously different.

"I can understand her anxiety," said Susanna softly. "But it isn't fair to blame Diablo for everything."

"What's going on? What are you guys doing here?" Harry came down the stairs, sleepily rubbing his eyes.

"We…ah…we wanted to have a cup of coffee together." Josh tried to give the boy an easy answer. "You should go back to bed. We promise to be really quiet," he said and smiled at Harry.

"Where's Ricki? Doesn't she want any coffee?"

"No! You know your Mom doesn't like it when she drinks coffee."

"Who? Mom?"

"No, silly! Ricki!" said Lillian. "But now get back to bed! I don't think your Mom will be very happy to see you up at this time of night," she added and then ushered the little boy gently toward the stairs.

"Okay. Good night, then." Harry walked back to the stairs and yawned. "When I'm big, I'm going to go on a night ride, too. I bet it's really cool," he said, and then he disappeared behind the banisters.

In the meantime, Marcus came back.

"Brigitte has finally gone to bed for a while. Her nerves

are shot," he said apologizing, and then he invited the whole group into the large kitchen.

"Sit down, everyone, the coffee will be ready in a minute. Anybody hungry? Lillian, Cathy, you know your way around here almost better than I do. Raid the refrigerator and find some bread. We'll make sandwiches. I think it would do us all good to eat something."

*

Kevin groaned with every step Diablo took, and Ricki had to force herself to keep going.

All these hours in her tight riding boots plus the unaccustomed night hike had made her feet swell, and she was beginning to get painful cramps in her calves. But she bit her lips and limped on. She tried with all her might not to think of the thunderstorm raging around them.

She led Diablo on a long strap and kept her hand buried in his wet mane. This way she could hold onto him and lean on his muscular neck for support while she tried not to slip on the wet, slippery path with her leather soles.

She wanted to use her imagination to get back to her daydream about the elves at Echo Lake in order to relieve the horror of her present situation, but suddenly she slipped on the wet stone trail Diablo had chosen and fell down.

Her scream startled Kevin, and Diablo also jerked and took a step sideways. The boy could hardly stay in the saddle.

With great presence of mind, he leaned forward and grabbed for the reins, which Ricki had had to let go of when she fell.

Diablo stood still while Kevin leaned toward Ricki. He could just hear a soft sobbing.

"Ricki? Are you okay? Ricki!"

The girl sat sniffling on the ground, massaging her ankle, which she knew was beginning to swell inside her boot.

"I can't go on!" Ricki was at the end of her strength. "I can't go on anymore!" she screamed. "Darn the night ride, darn this thunderstorm! I want to go home."

Sobbing from pain and desperation, she remained on the wet ground. Only Diablo's soft whinnying made her take a deep breath and try to stand up. But she just couldn't make it happen.

"Kevin, I can't get up. My ankle hurts so much. Kevin?"

The boy, who was still seeing everything spin in front of his eyes, was trying to get Diablo over to where Ricki sat. Although it was difficult in the darkness, he finally succeeded.

Ricki noticed that Kevin was trying to get down from her horse.

"For heaven's sake, stay there. I'll never get you back into the saddle again!"

"But you—"

"Stay up there!" repeated Ricki, this time louder than she really wanted to. Her thoughts were all jumbled. She had to quiet her mind if she were to think clearly.

All right, Ricki, she thought to herself, and with her eyes closed, she turned her face up toward the sky, as though the pelting rain could help her find a new perspective on the situation. *Kevin can't walk, and it doesn't look good for me either. Diablo needs to get home. I don't want him to get sick, too. God, what should I do?*

"Do you know where we are?" asked Kevin quietly, and Ricki shook her head.

"No idea," she admitted. "And I have no idea what time it is, or how many hours we're late. I'm sure the others are mad because I left the group. And when I think of my mother… Oh help, she's going to be furious with me."

Completely depressed, Kevin didn't say anything. *It's all my fault,* he thought sadly. If only the dizziness and the pounding in his head would stop so that at least he could help Ricki. The way it was now, he had to be glad if he didn't fall out of the saddle.

"Ricki?"

"What?"

"Ricki, I'm so sorry," he said softly. "We should have listened to you. You had a funny feeling about this ride right from the beginning, and I even laughed at you because of it. Please forgive me. Now I know that you were right to pay attention to your intuition."

Ricki tried once more to get up on her feet.

"Oh, forget about it! We can't change anything now, anyway. Ouch! What a mess!" Ricki managed to get up on one leg and was holding her swollen leg at an angle so as not to put any weight on it.

She looked around in all directions and then held her breath.

"Kevin! There's a car over there! That must be the road that goes past Echo Lake toward the town. There aren't any other roads around here."

Ricki was very excited. "If I'm right, that means we're not far from home!"

Kevin tried to find the headlights of the car as well, but for him everything was swirling in a thick fog before his eyes.

"If I could just put some weight on this ankle." Ricki

kept trying to take a small step, but it seemed to be impossible for her to make any progress like that.

"What if I get down and you leave me here?" asked Kevin. "Then you could ride home and send someone to pick me up."

"Are you crazy? I'm glad that I finally found you. I certainly don't feel like walking around looking for you at night again!"

"But—"

"Stop it! I don't want to hear anymore! Somehow we're going to get home together!" Ricki clamped her mouth shut and hopped over to her horse on her good leg. There she rested against him, completely drained.

Diablo turned his head toward her and rubbed his soft wet nostrils against her face.

"Oh, you," whispered Ricki. "I'm so glad that at least you're okay."

Diablo rubbed his forehead on her shoulder trustingly and almost made his owner fall down with his exuberant gestures of affection.

As Ricki petted her horse between the ears, an idea suddenly came to her. Was it possible that Diablo could carry them both?

"What do you think, sweetie, are the two of us too heavy for you? Oh, if only you could speak."

Diablo was getting restless. He didn't understand why the night walk had stopped. Tense, he stamped his hooves in place.

Couldn't these two young people see how close they were to their goal?

The horse whinnied again and shoved Ricki once more.

Come on! he seemed to say. *We've almost made it!*

Ricki sighed.

She felt bad that Diablo would now have to carry a double weight after being out all night on the trail, but she didn't see any other way to get home.

On the other hand, if she made him carry them only to the road, and then, yes! That's exactly what she would do!

"Take your foot out of the stirrup," she told Kevin, who looked down at her completely confused.

"What are you going to do?"

"You'll see in a minute. Diablo, stand still. I promise you, it's only for a very short distance!"

Awkwardly, and with a lot of pain in her throbbing ankle, Ricki managed to pull herself up behind the saddle.

Diablo laid his ears back and bucked with his hind legs. He didn't like it when his back was expected to bear more weight than just the saddle's. Ricki had noticed it several times before, when she had tried to put a saddlebag across the horse's back.

"Stay calm, sweetie, it's only me! Please, don't buck." Ricki tried to calm her horse, but Diablo seemed to be unsettled by the additional weight.

Dancing, he stepped to the right and then to the left, shaking his head in disapproval.

Ricki put her arms around Kevin, who leaned forward and held on to Diablo's mane for support. Now she wanted to guide her horse toward the road, but Diablo seemed to have a completely different idea and began to go in the opposite direction.

Ricki tried desperately to turn him around, but neither the nudges with her thighs, which were too far back anyway, nor the pulls on the reins had any effect. Too bad. She had thought that she could get off at the road and then send

117

Diablo home with Kevin. The animal would find his way from there easily without any help from Kevin. Then her father would come and pick her up right away.

She had to laugh at herself. Kevin would never have left her alone anywhere, but she, well, that was a different story.

She tried to coax her horse in the direction of the road, but Diablo remained stubborn, completely ignoring Ricki's instructions, which he normally followed without question. After a while, she gave up trying to influence her horse. She just didn't have the strength anymore, so she loosened her hold on the reins.

Undeterred, the black horse continued where his instincts were leading him. In the end, Ricki was glad that at least he had stopped bucking, trying to get rid of the weight on his back.

With tears in her eyes, she thought back to the road, which was getting farther away from them with every step Diablo took.

"Where are you taking us?" she asked her horse, all the while praying that he knew what he was doing.

Diablo, sensing that Ricki was no longer able to take charge, proceeded onward with conviction.

Chapter 8

"Thanks a lot, Mr. Sulai, that was great," Link smiled gratefully at Ricki's father. "The steaks we had before midnight didn't hold us very long, what with all the late-night activity. We were *really* hungry."

"This is good coffee, too," Susanna raised her mug, which she had refilled at least three times in the past hour.

Marcus left the coffee machine on, and Lillian and Cathy cleared the dirty dishes from the table. There were deep, dark circles under their eyes, and they could hardly keep their eyes open. It was already past 5 a.m., but they hadn't realized how late it was until they saw Jake standing in the doorway.

Jake was up that early every morning. He was used to it, because he always began working in the stable at 6 a.m.

Instead of his usual greeting, this morning he just nodded to Marcus and the others without saying a word. He could tell by the look on their faces that Ricki and Kevin were still missing.

...and Diablo, the old man thought, feeling a painful tugging at his heart. The animal meant more to him than anything else in the world.

119

Silent, he walked to the kitchen cabinet to get a coffee mug. Since his heart attack he wasn't supposed to have caffeine, but he insisted upon having at least one cup of coffee in the mornings. He said it was one of the few pleasures left to him.

Normally Brigitte kept him company at breakfast, but today she was conspicuously absent. Jake avoided asking about her and reacted only when Josh stretched and then got up from the table.

"I think we'd better get going," Josh said, and looked at the others. "It will be light out in half an hour and, to be honest, I can't stand sitting around doing nothing that long."

"Okay, let's begin a new round of searching." Revived by the strong coffee, Susanna got up, too, and was followed by the others.

Marcus regarded the young people with a heart full of gratitude.

"When Ricki and Kevin are back home safe and sound, we're going to have a gigantic barbecue, I promise! I don't know how I'll ever be able to thank you enough," he said a little embarrassed.

"A barbecue would be perfect, Mr. Sulai!" Ziggy smiled at him. "The main thing is that you're not mad at us anymore. It really wasn't our fault."

Marcus nodded.

"I know. Let's go!"

When they were almost out the door, Jake broke his silence. Quietly he asked, "Do you have a horse trailer with you?"

Josh stopped and laid a hand on the old man's shoulder.

"Don't worry, Jake," he said gently. "We haven't forgotten your Diablo. Ziggy's been driving all night with the trailer." He paused for a moment, then he added, "I promise you that we will bring Ricki, Kevin, and Diablo back home safely."

Jake didn't respond, he just turned his head to one side. *I hope you're right,* he thought to himself, while Josh joined the others.

"I hope I can keep my promise," Josh said softly, and took Lillian's hand. She had been waiting for him outside the door.

"Go back to bed," he said with a glance at Cathy, who looked like she was asleep standing up.

"But we want to help look for them, too!"

"You two are much too tired. "

"But we—"

"…and anyway, we have to keep the back seats empty for Ricki and Kevin when we find them."

Lillian understood, and so she sighed and gave her boyfriend a kiss. She watched him as he got into Robby's car.

"Can you go back to sleep?" asked Cathy. Lillian shrugged her shoulders.

"I don't know. I think Jake would really appreciate some help cleaning the stable, don't you?"

Cathy nodded.

"Okay. I'm not sure I'll be able to push the wheelbarrow in a straight line today, but you're right. Distraction is better than worrying or trying to get back to sleep and not being able to."

Together they returned to the kitchen to wash the plates and mugs, until Jake was ready to work in the stalls.

*

Ricki had wanted to dismount after a while, but she changed her mind.

Diablo didn't seem to mind the second weight on his back anymore, and he kept going without being hindered by the reins.

No matter where he goes, it will be fine, thought Ricki, trying to convince herself.

The storm had begun to abate, the rain was not as heavy as before, but that didn't change the fact that both riders were drenched, and trembled with the cold.

As the clouds moved away, the moon became partly visible.

"I can't believe it dares to shine after leaving us in the lurch all night," said Ricki, but Kevin didn't respond. He seemed to have dozed off in the saddle.

Now that they could see their surroundings a little better, Ricki recognized a small shrine at the edge of the trail and she knew immediately where they were.

She could have kissed Diablo, she was so happy.

These are Tom Anderson's fields! she thought, and felt a huge weight being lifted from her heart. *In just about another hour we'll be home! Heavens, we have been riding all over the place! We never should have come out of the woods here. I thought we were on the opposite side of the woods.*

Diablo whinnied softly.

See, Diablo seemed to say, *if you'd have let me have my head at the beginning, instead of pulling me to the left and the right, we would have been home a long time ago.*

"I understand, my good boy," murmured Ricki and stretched her tense back. "You'll get an extra portion of feed today for sure, no matter what Jake says. You've earned a reward!"

With every foot of progress they made, the moon seemed to retreat a bit more to make room for the sun, whose rosy colors were just becoming visible on the horizon.

Changing shifts, thought Ricki. She rubbed her eyes wearily with one hand. Luckily, daylight was not far off.

Now that she knew exactly where they were and what the trail looked like in front of them, she could breathe a sigh of relief. But although she was very happy that they had all survived the night, there was one worry that invaded her heart and her thoughts.

Where can Sharazan be? she kept asking herself, and hoped for Kevin's sake that nothing had happened to the roan.

"Please, dear God, don't take away another horse from him. He would never get over it. It was bad enough with Leonardo," she prayed quietly while gently stroking Kevin's back. She remembered the story about his first horse, which had to be put down.

With all that was on her mind, she still couldn't think of anything more glorious than the sight of the sun rising higher and higher in the sky. Its warm rays shined on the earth, which had taken such a beating from the storm, and on the two riders and their horse. It seemed like nature's attempt to make up for the terrifying night they had to endure.

That was really the night of all nights, she thought, and swore to herself for the umpteenth time that she would never go riding again if she had the slightest bit of anxiety about it.

Diablo stretched out his beautiful neck and almost touched the ground with it. He loved the smell of wet earth when the sun shone after a rain. Greedily, the animal breathed in the perfume of nature, then gave a big sneeze, shaking Ricki and Kevin, who were still on his back.

Ricki began to beam almost as brightly as the sun when she caught her first glimpse of the farms that were in her neighborhood. They didn't have much farther to go.

*

Lillian and Cathy dragged two bales of hay over to the stable door and sat down across from each other in the open doorway, their backs against the doorframe and their feet propped up on the other's bale. They stared into the distance, across the fields and meadows, hoping they would see the cars returning with Ricki and Kevin, and Diablo in the trailer.

The two girls had done almost all of Jake's work for him. They suspected that the old man's health wasn't too good.

Afterward, they had gone into the house with him, where they discovered Brigitte sitting at the kitchen table crying. There were mountains of used tissues lying all around her.

Harry sat next to her, quietly pushing his spoon around in his cereal bowl. He wasn't really hungry.

When Lillian and Cathy came in, he jumped up and ran over to the girls. Furious, he stood in front of them with his small hands clenched into fists.

"Why didn't you tell me that Ricki was missing? You should have told me last night! I could have gone out with Chico and helped with the search!" he yelled at them.

Lillian took a deep breath. "Look, Harry, just listen for a

124

minute," she began, but the young boy didn't let her finish the sentence.

"You guys are really mean! I'm sure I could have found Ricki!" His eyes glistened with anger.

"Harry, that's enough!" Jake took the boy, who fought back, and pushed him back to the table. "That's all we would have needed, for you to have gone riding, too! Look at your mother. Don't you think she has enough to worry about with Ricki missing? How do you think she'd feel if you were missing, too?"

Harry looked at his mother and felt terrible guilt. Her eyes were red and swollen from her tears.

"Yeah, I know, but—"

"No buts! Now eat!" Jake's voice was very firm, and Harry had the feeling that Jake wasn't going to take any opposition today.

The old man sat down beside Brigitte on the corner bench and put his wrinkled, sun-weathered arm around her.

Cathy and Lillian stood at the entrance to the kitchen for a while, unsure of what to do, and then left and went back to the stable.

*

Cathy stared at the road leading up to the Sulais' farmhouse as she slowly pulled out bits of straw from the bale on which she sat.

Hmm, she thought, *Jake and Ricki's mother don't have much to say today, but that's no wonder. One of them is worried about her daughter, and the other one about Diablo. I don't think there's much difference there. At least they find comfort sitting together silently.*

125

"If only I'd held on to Sharazan, none of this would have happened," Cathy scolded herself. She'd felt guilty about that all night.

Lillian tried to convince her friend that she wasn't responsible for the events of last night.

"It's not your fault that Rashid bucked because he was scared of the lightning. And anyway, who would have thought that Sharazan would just run away like that?"

"But if I'd let go of Rashid, then—"

"Then you might have had the problem of telling Carlotta that her horse was missing! No, Cathy, none of this is your fault." Lillian leaned forward and took her friend's hand. "You did the right thing. You were responsible for yourself and Rashid, and that's all!" she reminded Cathy. "Kevin is responsible for himself and Sharazan, just like everyone else is responsible for himself and his horse. I hope you can get that into your thick skull. If you have to blame anyone, then blame the weather for sending a flash of heat lightning at the worst possible moment. That's what spooked Rashid and Sharazan!"

Cathy slumped in silence. She knew that Lillian was right, but nevertheless…

"Look! They're coming back!" Lillian jumped up and ran into the yard.

Cathy followed her, although a little more slowly.

"Ziggy's car with the horse trailer isn't with them," she remarked softly.

"What?"

"The horse trailer, it's missing. That means Diablo isn't with them."

"Ohhhh," Lillian's joy at seeing the search party return was visibly dampened, and all at once she felt sure that

126

neither Ricki nor Kevin was in the back seat of any of the cars.

"Unsuccessful again," she mumbled, and felt sick to her stomach. It was past 6:30 a.m., as Marcus and their riding friends stopped their cars in front of the house. All of them were frustrated.

"Ziggy drove the trailer into a ditch," Josh shouted to the girls from a distance. "We had to pull it out and tow him back home."

Marcus, his shoulders hunched and with an anxious look on his face, walked over to the house. Most of the last hour had been spent getting Ziggy's vehicle out of the ditch and back home. Although it was very early Saturday morning, Marcus wanted to get in touch with his neighbors to see which of them would be willing to join the search for the kids at this hour. It had become clear to him that they needed a real search team to canvas the area systematically, and to do it in a much wider circle than they had done during the night.

*

Josh and his riding companions said good-bye to each other. They were going to drive home quickly and shower and change their clothes. Then they would meet back at the Sulais' farm and resume the search.

Lillian and Cathy remained in the stable by themselves. They were feeling useless and a little guilty for just standing around and not doing something to help.

"Come on," said Lillian suddenly. "Let's groom the horses, and maybe that will make the time go a little faster."

Cathy nodded in agreement. However, as much as they always enjoyed brushing the horses' coats to a sheen, today their motions were awkward, and the horses picked up their nervousness.

"Hey, what are you doing?" asked Lillian, a trifle irritated, as Rashid stepped sideways once again with his ears laid back and his nostrils flaring.

"I don't know," answered Cathy desperately. "Every time the horse moves, it makes me jump, and that gets Rashid so spooked that he's making me even more nervous. Ever since last night he's seemed completely different."

"No way! You're the one who's different. He senses your fears about Ricki and Kevin, and is instinctively reacting to them. Maybe it would be better if you put him back in his stall before you make him completely crazy."

Cathy swallowed hard. Lillian was right. If you're nervous, it's better not to handle a horse, otherwise something bad could happen.

"Don't worry about it. It'll get better," Lillian comforted her friend. She put Holli back in his stall, too.

"Come on," she said. "Let's go outside for a while. The fresh air will do us good. It'll clear our heads," she added, taking Cathy's arm and steering her gently toward the stable door. "A walk will be just the right thing. All we can do here is hang around and go nuts from waiting."

Without much enthusiasm, Cathy went along. Once back in the yard, Lillian asked sweetly, "Is there a particular place you'd like to go?" and Cathy answered,

"Yes. The place where we'll find Ricki, Kevin, and Diablo."

"Oh, Cath, if it were that easy, I'd have gone last night!" replied Lillian, and she squeezed her friend's arm in a gesture of empathy. "Come on, let's just walk around the house and across the field. It's quiet there and we won't see anyone at this hour of the day. You'll see, if we get ourselves calmed down, the world will look different to us."

*

Lillian had been right.

This wonderful area, through which the two girls were slowly walking, conveyed a feeling of peacefulness. There was almost nothing to remind them of the terrible storm of the past night. The sun was already warm enough to begin drying out the wet ground.

A few herons were walking gracefully over the meadow, undisturbed by the two girls walking near them, although several rabbits jumped out of sight. Here and there, butterflies fluttered among the wild flowers and bumblebees searched industriously for nectar.

"Isn't it beautiful here?" asked Lillian. She closed her eyes for a moment to enjoy the warm rays of the sun on her face. Cathy continued to look around.

Suddenly she grasped Lillian's arm.

"You're right," she laughed and shook her friend gently. "This is the most beautiful place in the whole wide world!"

Lillian opened her eyes and looked at Cathy, bewildered, as though she couldn't understand the sudden change in her friend's attitude.

"What happened? A little while ago, you were—"

Cathy stretched out her arm and pointed ahead. "There!"

"Where?"

"Up there! Don't tell me you don't see anything? Are you blind? C'mon!"

Cathy took off and raced ahead as though she had been stung by a wasp, pulling Lillian after her. Lillian shook her off and stopped so that she could see for herself what had caused Cathy's sudden excitement.

She gazed into the distance, and then she was running as fast as she could after Cathy.

They're back! she thought happily, and she started to laugh and cry at the same time, she was so relieved. *They're really back! Thank you, God!*

Cathy was almost out of breath, but she didn't want to stop to catch her breath. An unpleasant pain below her ribs made it hard for her to breathe, but she just pressed her hand against her side while she ran and hoped that the pain would go away as quickly as it had come.

"Rickiiii! Kevvinnnn!" she screamed, waving wildly at the two riders while she ran toward them.

Lillian had caught up with Cathy and waved both arms in the air. She couldn't get over how happy she felt.

Suddenly, she grasped Cathy's arm and stopped her abruptly.

"Something's wrong!" she panted. Her friend almost stumbled when she tried to stop suddenly.

"What?"

"Look at them closely! Ricki has to have seen us. Why doesn't she react? And if I'm seeing correctly, Kevin is more lying on Diablo's neck than sitting on his back."

Now Cathy saw, too.

"C'mon, we've got to keep going!" she urged.

The two of them had already used up all their energy in the short distance they had run. They could hardly breathe without chest pain, but they forced themselves to keep running toward the riders in the distance.

*

Ricki held the reins with one hand and tried to keep Kevin from falling off the saddle with the other.

Of course, she had seen her two girlfriends across the field, but she couldn't wave at them. She had to be careful that she didn't drop the reins and that Kevin didn't fall off. Nevertheless, she was really glad to see the two of them running toward her.

"Finally, we're back home," she murmured happily to herself, and let the tears of relief roll down her cheeks.

It was as though she couldn't believe she was actually here, in the golden sunlight, just a short distance from her home and family. She allowed here eyes to scan the horizon all around her, as though she had never seen this countryside before.

And she realized for the first time how beautiful it all was: golden yellow fields bathed in sunshine against the bright blue sky; dark green meadows with their varieties of grasses and flowers; the forest, which had now lost its terror for Ricki, and opened its gates between the trees for her. All of nature in its uniqueness seemed like the greatest miracle ever achieved on this planet.

Ricki felt as though she had been granted a new life after the horrific experience of last night.

She looked down at Kevin, who lay bent over Diablo's neck in front of her.

All during the long night she had thought about Kevin's condition, and had built an emotional wall between herself and him so that she wouldn't go crazy with worry. But now she was burned out and empty.

The fever Kevin had during the night seemed to have

risen, and Ricki was glad to have made it home so that he could get the medical care and rest necessary to recover from his ordeal. She was sure her parents would know what to do.

*

"Ricki...Ricki...where were you? Everyone's going crazy at home. Josh, Ziggy, Robby, and the others spent the whole night looking for you," burst out Cathy as she stopped dead in her tracks in front of Diablo.

"What happened to Kevin? God, he looks awful." Lillian stared at the boy's bright red face while she grasped Diablo's reins. Ricki was glad to let them go so that she could finally stretch a little.

"We have to get home immediately. Kevin had chills and fever last night. Please, quickly!"

Lillian nodded and led Diablo at a fast pace. She avoided further questions, and Cathy ran beside the horse, helping to support Kevin from below.

Ricki could finally let herself relax. She knew her friends would get them home safely. Exhausted, she closed her eyes and allowed her body to go with the rhythm of Diablo's gait.

You wonderful horse. What would we have done without you? she thought lovingly. *You have done so much for us, so often. I think no human could have done what you did. I love you so much.*

After a while she asked casually: "Sharazan?"

Lillian beamed back over her shoulder. "He's standing safe and sound in his stall. Susanna and Link caught him and Lisa drove him home."

"Lisa? Lisa Perkins? Did Albert allow that?" Ricki stared in amazement at her girlfriend below.

Cathy laughed.

"He was drunk! You were still there, weren't you? When we got to Echo Lake, Lisa ordered him into the car and drove him home. Afterward, she drove back with the horse trailer and was able to load Sharazan into it and take him home. Don't ask me where Susanna and Link found him. We haven't had a chance to ask them yet."

"Hmm," replied Ricki, somewhat distracted and not totally taking in all that Cathy was saying. She was staring at her home, which they were approaching rapidly, with her heart beating wildly.

She saw Jake, who was just leaving his cottage. She watched as he walked slowly across the yard and disappeared into the stable.

He probably can't stop worrying about Diablo, she thought sympathetically.

Diablo's head jerked upward. He whinnied loudly as he sensed his stable companions near, and from inside the stable came their answering neighs. To Ricki's ears, it was the most wonderful welcome she could wish for.

Chapter 9

From the tack room, Jake ran down the corridor and toward the stable door as fast as his stiff legs would allow. His long experience with horses told him that the animals hadn't become agitated for no reason.

When he saw his beloved Diablo with the two riders flanked by Lillian and Cathy about 150 yards from the house, he thought his knees would give way.

He kept trying to shout something to the kids, but he was too emotional to speak. He ran over to the house on shaky legs, opened the screen door and rang the doorbell continuously.

Marcus hurried to the door and opened it to find an overwrought Jake gesturing like a crazy person.

Excitedly, the old man kept pointing to the road leading to the front yard. Finally he was able to get out a few words.

"Ricki! Back!"

"WHAT?!" Marcus flew out of the doorway past Jake, bumping his elbow painfully on the doorframe, but he didn't seem to notice. His attention was riveted on the big black horse coming up the road and the two riders he was carrying.

"Brigitte!" he shouted back toward the house. "Brigitte! Ricki's back!" Then he ran toward Diablo, who just looked at him with surprise, as if to say, *Why are you making such a fuss?*

"Hi, Dad," said Ricki with a tired smile. "I'm fine," she added when she saw her father's concerned expression.

Carefully, she slid out of the saddle, but she flinched in pain when she put her weight on the sprained leg.

Marcus was able to catch her just before she began to stumble.

"It's just a sprain," Ricki hurried to explain. "But there's something wrong with Kevin. I think he hit his head on a rock, and then he lay outside for hours in the thunderstorm. I think he has a fever and chills, and, please, Dad…"

In the meantime, Brigitte had come running, too, and now she wrapped her arms around her daughter. She couldn't utter a word, and just held her tight.

"Bring Ricki inside," said Marcus. "I'll take care of Kevin."

While the girl limped and hopped toward the house supported by her mother's arm, Marcus carefully pulled Kevin down from the saddle.

Lillian and Cathy stroked Diablo and praised him extravagantly for bringing their friends home safely.

"You are a fantastic horse, do you know that? We're so proud of you!" Lovingly, Cathy patted his sweaty neck.

Kevin groaned, hardly able to take a step. Marcus took a breath, tensed his muscles, and then picked up Kevin and walked toward the house carrying him in his arms.

"Lillian, open the door for me, please," he said tersely, breathing heavily. The girl raced ahead and did as he asked.

With tears in his eyes, Jake took the black horse from

Cathy and led him to the stable, where he unsaddled the animal and tied him up in the corridor.

Diablo looked around him, as though he hadn't been here for years, and snorted excitedly. Chico was so happy to see him that he bellowed a loud donkey hee-haw. The other horses stretched their necks wide over the top of their stalls to greet their returned stable mate.

Jake made a large pile of oats in front of the horse and then walked slowly to the tack room, where he filled a bucket with warm water and dropped in a large sponge. Returning to his beloved Diablo, he began to wash down the horse.

"Can I help you with anything, Jake?" asked Cathy willingly, but the old man just shook his head. The girl realized that he wanted to be alone with Diablo, and so she walked away quietly.

Once outside, she ran over to the house to see how Ricki and Kevin were doing.

Her friend was sitting on a chair in the kitchen and Brigitte was just about to cut off the riding boots, although Ricki was protesting feebly. But it was impossible to get the swollen leg out of the boots any other way.

"Mom, please, they were so expensive," Ricki whined, partly in pain and partly in disappointment that her riding boots were about to be ruined.

"I know," answered Brigitte, her lips set in a hard line on her weary face. "I bought them." Cathy noticed that with the exception of that one comment, Brigitte was being very quiet.

Finally, Brigitte had Ricki's leg free.

"Oh, Mom, that feels so good," she sighed, now glad to be rid of the tight-fitting boot. But when her mother took off her riding pants and socks, Ricki shrieked.

The ankle, purple and blue with bruises, was also puffy and swollen.

"You have to see the doctor," Brigitte decided, but Ricki emphatically shook her head no.

"Nonsense! It's just a sprain! Where's Kevin?"

"That doesn't look like just a—"

"Mom," she began again, "I'm sorry, but I couldn't just ride back home and leave Kevin. I had the feeling that he—"

"I have a feeling, too," interrupted Brigitte a little more brusquely than she'd intended. "I have the feeling that your horse only brings you bad luck. Ever since you got Diablo, you go from one misadventure to another, and I can't stop worrying about you!"

"But, Mom, Diablo is a wonderful horse. He—"

"If you didn't have your own horse, you would never have thought about participating in that moonlight ride!"

Cathy felt that she had to help her girlfriend, and so she said, "Excuse me, Mrs. Sulai, but I don't have my own horse and I—"

Brigitte threw her an angry glance. "If I want to hear your opinion, I'll ask you, Catherine!"

Cathy stepped back suddenly, as if she were slapped, and Ricki began to tense up as well. When her mother called people by their formal names, she knew there was going to be trouble.

"Mom, please."

"I'm going to ask Jake to take Diablo back," said Brigitte, as she put together an ice pack to take the swelling down.

"NO!" Ricki screamed. The thought of having to give up Diablo was just too much for her strained nerves. "If you do that…" She stared at her mother with tears in her eyes.

"Then what? What happens if I do?" Brigitte's eyes were sharp.

"Then, then, I'll leave!"

"Oh? Do you see? That's how far it's gone already. That horse can actually get you to leave home! Isn't that just terrific!"

"That *horse* doesn't do anything!" Ricki shouted furiously. "You do it all by yourself! You're so mean. The truth is Diablo found Kevin, he carried us throughout the night, and he brought us safely home, after I gave him his head to find the right way. I was completely confused, I lost all sense of direction, and I made him walk in circles for hours. And now, after he brought us safely home, you want to take this wonderful horse away from me? Never! Do you hear me? Never!" Ricki tried to get up on her feet.

"Just because *you're* afraid of horses, you want to take Diablo away from *me*. That's just not fair." Ricki was sobbing so loudly that even Harry stuck his head in the doorway.

"What's going on?"

"Out!" Brigitte shoved him back out the door, but before she could say anything further to her daughter, Ricki hobbled past her, obviously in a lot of pain.

"Ricki! You stay put!" Brigitte angrily ordered her daughter, but Ricki didn't even turn to look at her. She managed to reach the door where Cathy stood, an uncomfortable witness to this mother-daughter quarrel, and leaned on her friend's shoulder. The look of sadness on Ricki's face was so profound that Cathy felt just awful for her girlfriend.

In silence, the two teens left the kitchen.

When they were gone, Brigitte sank into a chair and,

138

with her hands cradling her head on the table, cried softly to herself.

What have I done? she thought desperately. *Instead of embracing my daughter and telling her how glad and happy I am that she's finally home, I add even more pain to the horrible night she experienced. But that horse! Ricki just shouldn't ride anymore. The worry and fear that something will happen to her are going to kill me one day.*

*

Lillian stood next to the sofa where Marcus had laid Kevin. Ricki's father nervously paced back and forth holding his cell phone. He had dialed the number again and again, but kept getting a recording asking him to leave a message.

"You would think there would be someone at the doctor's office to answer the phone! But I guess they hope no one needs medical attention on the weekend!"

Frustrated that he couldn't reach the doctor in person, he finally left his name and number on the answering machine, telling the doctor that it was an emergency.

After what seemed like an eternity, but was actually only a few minutes, the phone rang. Marcus described the situation briefly and concisely to Dr. Clemens and the doctor promised to come by within the half-hour.

"Wrap the boy in two or three blankets, give him something to drink—as much as he wants—and put a cold compress on his injured leg. Can you do that? Good. I'll hurry."

*

Marcus shut off the phone and left the room to speak to Brigitte. On his way out, he motioned to Lillian, pointing to a few blankets folded up on one of the armchairs. "Please, cover Kevin up well. I'll be right back.

In the hallway, he saw Ricki coming toward him. She was crying so hard that she could barely breathe. Lovingly he took her in his arms.

"What's wrong, sweetheart?" he asked, and because Ricki was too distraught to speak, Cathy told him about the argument.

He listened with increasing dismay, then shook his head sadly. Now that his wife had said what he himself had thought for one brief moment during the night, he realized that he was partly to blame for Ricki's unhappiness. Objectively, he had to admit that sometimes the horse seemed like a guardian angel. Marcus thought back to the fire at the riding academy. Diablo had been a major factor in saving the lives of Jake and the horses.

No, he thought. *We shouldn't use that horse as an excuse to cover up for our own insecurities and failures. Diablo is—*

He couldn't continue with his thought. Ricki grabbed onto his arm and, sobbing, pleaded: "Dad, she just can't take Diablo away from me. Please tell me that she can't do that. I, I…"

Marcus stroked the hair from his daughter's eyes and smiled at her gently.

"No one is going to take Diablo away from you. I promise."

"But Mom, she—"

"Not Mom either," said Marcus firmly, finally stopping Ricki's tears.

"I'll talk with her, but you, little girl, get to bed now. I have to get your mother to make a cold compress for

140

Kevin's leg." Then, turning to Cathy, he asked, "Cathy, could you get him something to drink? The doctor said he should drink as much as he can."

"Of course, Mr. Sulai." Cathy let go of Ricki. "I'll be right back," she said and disappeared in the direction of the kitchen. Before she went in, she took a deep breath to prepare herself for Brigitte's anger, which had been directed toward her, too. Ricki's mother, however, just sat quietly at the kitchen table and acted as though she didn't even see Cathy.

"Ahmm, I'm supposed to get something for Kevin to drink," she said softly. Brigitte just pointed at the fridge, without looking up.

"I know how to make cold compresses, too! I can't sleep now anyway," Ricki was just saying to her father, who had brought her to Kevin as she had asked him.

"All right," said Marcus. "Your mother won't be angry if you take over this part. What do you need?"

"Two towels, one plastic bag slit open, a bowl of cold water, and if possible, ice cubes in the water," she answered with confidence, and she had to smile as her father saluted her.

"Aye, aye, ma'am. I'll get everything immediately!" he replied, and quickly left the living room.

*

Kevin lay in the darkened guestroom, the curtains having been drawn. The doctor had diagnosed him as having a slight concussion, a bad flu with a high fever, and a number of bumps and bruises.

"His ankle looks much worse than it is," he said, relieved, after thoroughly examining Kevin. "All he needs is few days of rest, of lying in bed, taking the medicine that I prescribed for him, and some loving care from you." He smiled at Ricki knowingly. She lowered her eyes in embarrassment, but was very relieved to hear his diagnosis.

"Now, let's have a look at my other patient," he said, motioning for Ricki to sit down. He undid the elastic support bandage she had wrapped around her ankle and gently moved her foot up and down, side to side, and around. Carefully he felt along the ankle joint.

"Well, the good news is the tendons in your foot are a little sprained, and quite painful, I know, but it's not serious. The salve I left on the table should do the trick. Rub it in several times a day."

Ricki still looked concerned. "And the bad news?" she asked.

"You shouldn't do any hiking for a while," joked the doctor. "Elevating the leg will help the most, so I want you to stay off your feet as much as possible."

Ricki rolled her eyes, but she nodded in submission at the doctor's words.

"So, if everything is cleared up now, I think I'd better get going," he said. Marcus shook his hand gratefully and went with him to the door.

"The two of them were really lucky," Dr. Clemens said to Ricki's father when they were out of Ricki's earshot. He watched the girl sit down carefully on the edge of Kevin's bed and grasp his hand.

"Such a stupid thing to do, riding in that kind of weather, and at night."

Marcus avoided any explanations, preferring not to react to what the doctor had just said. He didn't feel like listening to the doctor's accusations about him allowing his daughter to go on the ride.

At the front door, Marcus shook the doctor's hand. "Many, many thanks for your help, Doctor," he said in a friendly voice. He watched as Dr. Clemens got into his car before he closed the door.

For a moment, Marcus leaned his back against the door, wondering what he should do first. Then he straightened up and disappeared into his study.

First I'll call Kevin's mother to let her know what's been happening, he thought, looking for the slip of paper Kevin had given him that had the phone number of the spa where Caroline Thomas and Carlotta were spending the weekend.

"Ah, here it is!"

He decided to talk to Brigitte about Diablo later.

"Diablo, yes, I'll go see him, too, afterwards, and thank him for everything," he said softly to himself as he reached for the phone and dialed the spa's number.

Then he remembered that he had to inform Ricki's other riding companions about his daughter's and Kevin's safe return so that they could stop looking for them. *But what are their last names or phone numbers?* he asked himself as he focused on a picture of Ricki that stood on his desk. *For the moment, it will have to take a back seat to what's happening here.*

*

While Kevin was asleep, Ricki hobbled over to the stalls where she was received with enthusiastic hugs from Lillian and Cathy.

"Hey, we haven't seen you for a long time," laughed

143

Lillian, and Cathy joked: "Oh yeah, ride all night and then you don't even take care of your horse. We really appreciate that!"

Ricki grinned. "That's what you think!" she responded, and went straight to the big feed bin and got a bowl full of oats.

"Be careful that Jake doesn't catch you with that," warned Lillian. "You know how much he hates extra rations!"

"Today I just don't care," Ricki replied as she shuffled slowly over to her horse. "I promised Diablo a reward and he's going to get one! Jake can just lump it!"

"If you think that I'm going to mind, you're wrong," said a familiar gruff voice coming from the doorway. The old stable master came inside and looked fondly at the girl and the wonderful black horse, who looked none the worse for wear from the adventure of the previous night.

The horse chewed on the delicious oats while nodding his head as if to say: *I like this! You could give me extra portions more often!*"

"You're right, he really earned it. Tell me, where did you two go last night?" asked Jake, his eyes squinting.

"Yeah, I'd like to know, too," added Lillian.

"We're all curious," Cathy added.

Ricki stroked her horse's head tenderly and began to recall all the things that had happened.

"Well, it was like this…" she began, and three pairs of eyes concentrated on her as she began her story.

*

The following days were filled with peace and quiet and sleep, which revived Ricki's and Kevin's energy.

Kevin's fever had gone down and the horrible headaches had gone away. He sat happily in bed, although he was often bothered with bad bouts of coughing. He used up huge amounts of tissues and cough drops, which were regularly supplied by his mother, who, after receiving Marcus's phone call, had returned with Carlotta later that same day.

Since the boy had been quite ill, Marcus had insisted that he could stay in the guestroom until he had recovered. Therefore, Kevin's mother had moved in as well, so that she could take care of her son and not inconvenience the Sulais any more than necessary.

While in his feverish delirium, Kevin kept calling for Sharazan, and his friends assured him that his beloved horse was safe and sound in his stall.

Ricki was, of course, very happy that her boyfriend now practically lived in the room next to hers, and she spent more time sitting at his bedside than she did in the stable.

Nevertheless, she kept slipping out to see to her Diablo as well as Sharazan, who was moping because he missed Kevin.

"Kevin will come as soon as he can," she tried to explain to the roan, but he kept staring at the door as if he couldn't understand why the boy didn't come to see him.

*

The minute the dizzy spells that had continued to plague Kevin stopped, there was no holding him down.

"I have to go to Sharazan, otherwise he won't remember who I am," he tried to convince his mother. "I haven't seen him since the night ride!"

Reluctantly, Caroline Thomas gave in. She knew that

145

seeing Sharazan would probably do Kevin more good than staying in bed against his will.

"Just don't overdo it in the stalls," she instructed Kevin, but he laughed.

"Sure, Mom. First of all, I'm going to clean out all the stalls, then unload a cart of hay, and then I'll play Frisbee with the bales," he teased her with a grin.

Ricki gave him a pretend dirty look as they left the room together.

"Is that any way to speak to your mother?" she asked smiling, gently poking him in the arm.

"You're a fine one to say that, after what I heard happened between you and your mother."

"Oh, that's all in the past," Ricki said, dismissing her friend's words. "Dad talked to her. She was just upset and frantic with worry. But she's come around. She's made her peace with Diablo and, thank goodness, there's no longer any talk of me having to give him up."

They walked across the courtyard to the stable.

"Terrific, then everything is okay!" Kevin was relieved, and Ricki noticed that the closer he got to the stable, the more confident he was on his legs.

It was easy for her to understand her friend. She wouldn't have felt any differently.

Touched, she watched as Sharazan hammered against the stall gate with his hooves and whinnied again and again in sheer joy at seeing Kevin.

The boy opened the door to the stall and embraced the horse's neck.

"I missed you so much," he said softly, and pulled out a few sugar cubes he'd taken from Brigitte Sulai's sugar bowl.

Marcus kept his word. The next week he told Ricki to call all the riders who had searched for her and Kevin untiringly throughout that long, stormy night. The promised "thank-you barbecue" was finally going to take place.

"Come Saturday, please, about 3 p.m., and bring an appetite and your good humor," said Ricki. "Dad is going to grill steaks and kabobs and burgers and hot dogs, and Mom is creating mounds and mounds of salads. With all that food, the best thing to do is just have a light breakfast and skip lunch, so we won't have too much left over from the barbecue."

All of them said they would love to come, except Lisa, who hesitated.

"You know, Albert," she mumbled, when Ricki called to invite her, but Ricki answered honestly and directly, as always: "I realize that he's your husband, but I don't care what he thinks. Lisa, you're very important to all of us!"

The young woman was silent.

After a few moments, Ricki said, "Well, think about it, and if you want to come, then just come. We would all be happy to see you and it would be great to have you here!"

When she hung up, she stared at the receiver for a while. *Albert has a very sweet wife. I wonder when he's going to realize that,* she thought, before she dialed the next number.

*

The day of the barbecue was picture perfect. The sun had been shining all morning, and it made the bright sky seem more intensely blue than ever.

"It looks like the weather will hold," commented Marcus, looking out the window. He was dipping the steaks into his secret marinade so they would be tender and ready for the grill that afternoon.

The four teenagers were cutting up vegetables for the shish kabobs. Ricki had made Kevin peel and chop a huge pile of onions. While he was suffering with burning, watering eyes, Brigitte was busy preparing one salad after another.

"Tell me, Dad," began Ricki quietly, when she was sure that her mother wasn't listening. "Do you think I have Clara's gift for second sight?"

Marcus shook his head. "To be honest, I don't think you have her gift. If you did, then you wouldn't have had to search for Kevin or your way home for hours on end," he answered in a low voice.

Ricki heaved a sigh of relief. "Well, I'm glad. I don't think it's so great to know everything in advance."

Turning to Brigitte, and the huge bowls of delicious-looking salads that took up most of the table, she asked, "Wow, Mom, who's going to eat all that?" as she helped herself to a spoonful of the sweet-and-tangy red-pepper salad.

"Me!" chimed in Harry, who was watching closely. He became furious when everyone burst out laughing. Insulted, as he always was when he felt people were making fun of him, he decided not to hang around the kitchen anymore, so he left to play with Chico.

When the guests began to arrive that afternoon, however, Harry was the first one to run to tell them, even before they were out of their cars, about all of the fabulous things they were about to eat.

Kevin had already fired up the barbecue, and Brigitte

148

had spread out the salads and bowls of potato chips and fruit under the enormous patio umbrella.

The beverages were chilling in the so-called summer refrigerator, which the Sulais had put in the little room off the patio back in June. They planned to leave it there until the beginning of cooler weather, then move it to the basement.

"Hey, I'm so glad you came!" Ricki beamed as she accepted a large bouquet of flowers from Susanna and thanked her.

"This is for you from all of us," Susanna said, and then she held out another bouquet. "And this is for your mother. Where is she?"

Ricki pointed toward the house.

"I think she's in the kitchen. You know the way."

Susanna nodded and disappeared into the house while Ricki thanked each of the guests for the lovely flowers. Then she went to find a large vase to put them in.

She was especially glad to see Lisa, who arrived a half-hour later.

Happily, the four friends ran over to her and each gave her a hug. They were all quite astonished when Albert drove up a little while later.

"What does he want here?" asked Kevin, surprised, and Ricki just shrugged her shoulders.

"I have no idea, but if he came just to bother us that will really make me mad. I had enough of that at the barbecue that night," she growled though clenched teeth.

As Albert slowly walked toward the others, who were already sitting together and having a good time, everyone grew quiet. All you could hear was the fire crackling in the grill.

Lisa turned pale when she saw her husband. He was visibly embarrassed. Unsure of what to expect, she got up awkwardly and slowly walked over to him.

"What are you doing here?" she asked him a little nervously. She wished she had stayed home. She couldn't stand it if he ruined everyone's good time and embarrassed her again.

"I . . . I . . . wait . . . "

Quickly he produced two small bunches of sweetheart roses, a red one and a yellow one, from behind his back.

"What's he up to?" Cathy wondered, but before Lillian could make any juicy comment, Albert stepped over to his wife and held out the red roses to her.

Loudly, so that everyone could hear him, he said earnestly: "I want to apologize to my wife for my behavior, and I want all of you to be witnesses when I promise here and now never to drink alcohol again. I know it won't be easy and I realize that I'll need help, professional help, to be able to keep my promise. But I know in my heart that I will succeed. I have too much to lose if I don't!"

"Hear, hear," whispered Josh.

"Shut up!" warned Lillian. "I want to hear what else he has to say."

"It's taken me a long time, but I've come to realize that I have a truly wonderful wife, who, thankfully, didn't allow me to bully her, and against my wishes went back out during that thunderstorm to help search for Ricki and Kevin. Lisa, I'm sorry for all the hurtful things I've done and said to you over the years, and I beg you to forgive me."

Lisa had tears in her eyes as she threw her arms around her husband's neck. At last, here was the nice guy she had married six years ago, and she saw in his public apology a new chance to find happiness again in her marriage.

The riders applauded, but Albert gestured for them to stop.

Gently he removed Lisa's arms and stepped over to Ricki, who had a funny "what-now?" feeling in the pit of her stomach.

Lisa must have felt the same way, she thought, as Albert handed her the bouquet of miniature yellow roses.

"I want to apologize to you, too, with all my heart. I called you some pretty nasty names. If I could, I would take them all back. After what I heard about you, you deserve my greatest admiration. You are braver than all of us put together. Not one of us had the courage to go searching for Kevin on horseback during the thunderstorm that night. You know that it was really dangerous, and I hope you never do that again. But still, my hat's off to you, and I'm glad that you found Kevin in time."

Ricki blushed with embarrassment. She didn't like to be praised like that in public, but she was glad, of course, that Albert seemed to have changed completely.

She nodded her thanks to him and pointed over to the picnic tables and chairs that Marcus had set up.

"Sit down, Mr. Perkins, and have something to eat. There are plenty of steaks—and you don't have to get in line here at our house," she said with a huge grin. Albert knew exactly what she was referring to.

"I acted like an idiot!" he said dejectedly, and then he smiled back at Ricki. "I promise, it will never happen again. By the way, please call me Albert. Forget that 'Mister Perkins' stuff. Okay?"

"Fine, Mister…er….Albert." Ricki reached out and shook his hand and realized that this man wasn't unpleasant—when he wasn't drinking alcohol.

While Albert took Lisa's hand and went to sit down with the others, Ricki went into the house to find vases for the two bouquets of roses.

When she got back, Kevin came toward her carrying a gigantic gift basket overflowing with apples, carrots, horse treats, a few sugar cubes, and a huge box of chocolates.

Ricki put the flowers on the picnic tables and turned to him. "What's that?" she asked, her gaze shifting between Kevin and the basket.

He smiled shyly. "That's my thank-you for the heroine of the night who found me, and, with great effort, brought me home safely." Kevin leaned over and gave Ricki a loving kiss on the cheek.

Embarrassed, but incredibly and indescribably happy, Ricki grabbed an apple and bit into it.

"I'm right, aren't I, that the box of chocolates is for Diablo and the rest is for me?"

As Ricki laughed heartily, she heard Diablo whinnying his protest loudly from the stable.